HAMILTON JOBSON

To Die a Little

St. Martin's Press,
New York

Copyright © 1979 by Hamilton Jobson
All rights reserved. For information, write:
St. Martin's Press
175 Fifth Avenue
New York, N.Y. 10010
Manufactured in the United States of America

Library of Congress Catalog Card Number: 78-69744

ISBN 0-312-80565-6

CHAPTER I

My introduction to Hannaford was both dramatic and amusing. The drama came when the foot-bridge guardrail on which I was leaning suddenly gave way and I was precipitated into the deeper part of the river.

I had gone for a stroll, had stopped on the bridge for a while and, after an interesting few minutes gazing down at the dark trout snaking about in the water below, I turned and practically sat on the rail as I admired the scenery. It was typically English: the winding river with its shades of green and blue, swift-running water smoothing in places towards inlets which held reeds and water-lilies, grassy banks and trees of enchanting variety. It was all very quiet and peaceful.

I pulled out my pipe and was filling it when it happened. Being nearly six feet tall, the rail was wedged comfortably under my buttocks. I suppose I am a little overweight – although fourteen stone isn't excessive – and perhaps I was leaning back further than was advisable. If I had been expecting it I could have saved myself, for the rail didn't disintegrate. With a protesting creak, it sagged outwards and the top half of my body immediately began to pivot on the fulcrum supplied by my bottom and the rail. For a few seconds my legs and arms thrashed the air as I made a vain attempt to fall the right side of the rail, but all I succeeded in doing was to overbalance still further and no doubt make myself look ridiculous into the bargain.

I had gone down head first and somehow I managed to surface the right way up, spluttering and spitting out water and snorting through my stinging nose. Then I panicked, and not without cause. I can't swim and my feet were nowhere near touching bottom. It's all very well receiving advice about keeping calm and moving slowly and so on, but you need practice and I'd never bothered to get any. I splashed around wildly, went down and up again. I tried to hold my breath when I went down for the second time but I choked and seemed to swallow half the river.

God knows what would have happened then, but a pair of strong hands appeared from nowhere to grab me under the armpits and I was propelled backwards with my head just above the surface. I still spluttered and spat out water but I had the sense not to struggle any more, and within seconds I was being hauled on to the bank.

I lay there coughing and panting but I managed to gasp out, 'Thanks, whoever you are.' Then I moved my head to see what my rescuer was like. My eyes first rested on a pair of wet, brown brogue shoes and travelled upwards to sodden, brown slacks and shirt clinging to a tall, athletic male body.

Then a voice said, 'Bloody good job you weren't crossing Niagara Falls on a one-wheeled bicycle!' Despite the traumatic experience of only a few minutes previously, this struck me as decidedly funny and I leaned further back to get his head in focus. It was an interesting face, one which you wouldn't lose in a crowd. The features were definite and well formed, the wide mouth good-humoured, the eyes under thickish brows were steady and friendly, with tell-tale crowsfeet at the edges. His hair, which now streaked wet from his forehead, was brown and not too thick except for little tufts above the ears. Having said all that, the most apt description, I suppose, is that his facial balance and expression went very well with his voice: easy and lazy in a cultured sort of way. I put his age at anything from forty to fifty.

Limp strings of green weed stuck to him and water still dripped from him. He passed a large, elegant hand across his forehead, sweeping back his hair, and then he added, 'You seem all right, Captain. Didn't swallow too many fish, I hope?'

I struggled to my feet, shook myself a bit and pushed my hair back as he had done.

'I can't swim.'

'I gathered that. Mind you, your acrobatics before the plunge were worth seeing. I wish I'd had my cine-camera with me.'

'I'd have drowned if you hadn't come along.'

He nodded soberly. 'You might have, at that. A horrible thought struck me as I was towing you in – were you the income tax man? I say, you're not, are you?'

His mood was infectious and I laughed.

'Far from it. But look here, it's not really a joking matter. I could easily be dead. You deserve a medal or something. The Royal Humane Society, isn't it?'

He gave me a rather old-fashioned look and then walked a few yards away and picked up a green-check sports jacket he'd obviously left there before he had dived in.

'I've got my car up at the top,' he said. 'How far have you got to go for a rub down and change?'

'Less than half a mile,' I said. 'How about you?'

'Bulford. About fifteen miles.'

'Well . . . The least I can do. Come to my place and I'll lend you something to get home in. We're about the same size.'

He pondered on this. 'What about your wife? It won't take me all that long to get back.'

'There's no one except me. There's a bath and shower and a double scotch, if you want it.'

'Now you're talking! Only one thing, though. You don't mention this to anyone.'

'But . . .'

'I mean it. No one. You won't be doing me any favours, quite the opposite. Promise me that first.'

I shrugged. 'If you insist. But I feel I ought to repay you in some way . . . express my appreciation. God, man! I could be dead.'

'You've already said that. You owe me nothing. Didn't you know that saving other people's lives makes you feel good? Anyway, is it a promise?'

'Reluctantly, I promise.'

He stared hard at me. 'I like the look of you. I take you for a man of your word. The name's Hannaford, Tom Hannaford.'

'John Bryant,' I said.

We shook hands and then climbed the bank to the road.

The car was parked in a natural lay-by in the lane above and when I saw it I reflected that, if he hadn't borrowed it, he must be more than comfortably off. It was a gleaming, wine-coloured Mercedes sports and by its condition and the last letter on the registration plate, it was new or as good as.

'We're rather wet to get in there,' I said.

He squelched round to the boot. 'Not to worry. Hold fast a bit.'

With that he produced a thin canvas sheet which he draped over the seats. It seemed made for the job.

'Okay,' he said. 'In you get and lead me to your hideaway.'

Perhaps his reference to my four-roomed thatched cottage as a 'hideaway', which as far as I knew he had never seen, was unconsciously apt. Although, as I came to know him better, I found that sometimes he revealed an uncanny instinct for making deadly accurate assumptions. I had in fact bought it just over a year previously for the purpose of hiding away, as it were. It was square and white, with perhaps more than its share of slatted windows for the period it represented. There was an unpretentious garden of lawn and shrubs, and a winding brick path which led up to a separately-thatched porch with honeysuckle trailing up the sides. Only the garage, with a drive-in well to the left, and the telephone wires gave any indication of the age we lived in.

Inside I had made a few alterations without destroying the character of the place, and the sitting-room, with its inglenook fireplace and furniture which I had chosen with great care, had a warm, welcoming atmosphere. Central heating had been installed but I still used the open fire in winter.

Hannaford made no comment until I was leading him up the angled stairway from the square hall.

'This is really charming,' he said.

I showed him the bathroom. 'There's a clean towel there. I'll sort out some clothes for you and leave them outside the door. I don't know about shoes. Perhaps a pair of slippers would be the best idea. I'll lend you some.'

'What about you?' he asked.

'I'll have a rub down and change in the kitchen. Come down when you're ready.'

He stood just inside the bathroom, nodding appreciatively. 'Very kind of you,' he said.

It didn't take me long to dry off and change, and I was waiting for him when he appeared at the sitting-room door. The slacks I'd let him have were a bit baggy at the waist and hips and the shirt a trifle tight across the shoulders, but otherwise they weren't a bad fit. He was carrying his own wet clothes and shoes rolled into a bundle.

'I'll take these and leave them in the porch, shall I?' he said.

'That'll be fine. What'll you have to drink and how d'you like it?'

'You mentioned a double scotch. Don't spoil it with anything.'

He was back by the time I had poured and, with a drink in his hand, he eased into a chair and crossed his legs. Then he raised his glass.

'Here's to luck and to you, of course.'

I raised my own. 'Here's to you, with my deepest gratitude. If there's anything within my limited means I can do for you at any time, don't hesitate to ask.'

I had noticed by now that there seemed to be a permanent twinkle in his eyes. It was not the look of sardonic amusement that some people like to adopt, but rather a genial expression of good fellowship. Within minutes he had made himself completely at home. He could have been an old friend who had just dropped in.

I sat in the chair opposite. 'Is there anyone you want to phone?' I asked. 'Your wife or somebody?'

'No. She won't be expecting me for a while. Thanks all the same.' He glanced slowly round the room. 'What a delightful house you have here. I presume it is yours?'

'Yes. I bought it a year last February and I must say I find it a bit of a change from City life.'

'It's just the sort of place my wife would like.'

'Bring her over some time. Just give me a ring so I'll be sure to be in.'

'I'll do that.' He lifted his glass and surveyed the remains of the clear amber liquid. 'This is the real McCoy. I'd say Glenlivet or . . .'

'You had it first time. I use a cheaper brand normally but I always keep a couple of bottles handy for special occasions. I don't think you could have a more special occasion than this.'

He put his glass down. 'You and your house – they intrigue me. Tell me to mind my own business, but what d'you do exactly?'

'I'm retired.'

I've been told that I look younger than my forty-five years and I saw the question mark appear on his forehead.

'It was an early retirement. I was, and still am, I suppose, an architect. With the same firm for twenty-two years. But I'd better put you in the picture. My wife died nearly two years ago and I'm afraid I rather went to pieces.' It occurred to me that he was the first person I'd voluntarily confided in since then, and for some reason I actually wanted to tell him. 'I've got over it now. I have a reasonable pension from the firm, and on top of that there's a legacy from my father which has left me more than enough to get by. At the time I felt I had to move right away and when I found this place I knew it was made for me.'

'So you don't do anything now?'

'I'm not gainfully employed, if that's what you mean. I had an extension made at the back here where I paint. I've always dabbled with it but now I have more time. I read a lot and most days I spend an hour down at our local pub.'

'You're an artist?'

'With limitations. It's only a hobby.'

'Any children?'

'No.'

'Don't you ever get lonely?'

'Not often. Sometimes I do, but . . .' I shrugged. 'It's the price you pay for the compensations of a place like this and frankly I'd sooner have my own company than somebody else's forced upon me.'

I noticed that his glass was empty and pointed to it. 'Another?'

'I'd like another, as long as you won't think I'm forcing my company on you.'

'That was tactless of me. I didn't mean it that way, I assure you. You are more than welcome. Stay as long as you like.'

I refilled his glass and, as I handed it to him I checked the time. 'It's now five to six. Would you care to join me in a meal about eight?'

'I'd like to but I'd better not. My wife will be expecting

me by half past seven at the latest and she'll have something ready.'

We both had another drink and went on chatting like old friends. One thing puzzled me, not so much then as later. When, thinking of his pricey car, I asked him, 'What's your line of business?' he gave a somewhat mischievous grin and said, 'It could be crime for all you know!'

I assumed that this was his way of keeping it to himself and I laughed to avoid embarrassment.

'That certainly seems to pay these days,' I said.

'I'd like to see this studio of yours.'

I stood up. 'All right. Bring your drink with you.'

The extension is reached from a door in the kitchen. It is roughly fifteen feet by ten and to a height of about five feet is of brick, the rest being of reinforced opaque glass, the roof as well, except for a few clear panes to offset any claustrophobic effect.

My easel, with a half-finished landscape, stood at one end. There were two bentwood chairs, a large cabinet where I kept my materials and a long bookshelf. Some of my stuff, devoid of outer frames, was hanging on the walls and some stood piled against one wall. The floor, grey-and-white tiles, was as I expected very clean. Mrs Simmonds had been in that morning and although she could neglect other places she had a thing about floors.

He looked first at the canvas on the easel and then at the paintings on the wall. I let him browse and watched him. With an occasional sip at his glass, he studied each one very seriously and eventually went to the pile against the wall. 'D'you mind?'

'Help yourself,' I said and, as he turned them for inspection, added, 'One thing you should know. I'm not much good at anything original. They're nearly all copies.'

His head came up and he said, 'Copies?'

'All but two of them.'

He went back to one on the wall. 'This a copy?'

'Yes. I'm rather pleased with that. It's from a picture on last year's calendar.'

'I'd like to compare it with the original.'

It was in a drawer in the cabinet. I got it for him and he stood comparing it. 'It's good, bloody good. My friend, you're wasting your talents.'

I pointed to one against the wall. 'That's an original. Not much talent there. I can never get the perspective quite right and the rest, I think, is amateurish.'

'Okay, but you can copy. You've enlarged the original here – what, ten times? – and the end result is something anybody would like.' He gave me back the calendar picture. 'If I could get you fifty pounds in cash for every painting of that standard, would you take it on?'

'You mean you could get fifty pounds for that, a copy?'

'In a decent frame I'd get seventy-five to a hundred.'

'Where?'

'In my shop. I've an antique shop in Northminster.'

'Is it near a corner, double-fronted with large bow windows? If so, I've passed it in the car.'

'That's it. Think about it. You needn't declare anything to the income tax people. How long would one of these take you?'

'Two or three days. Depends how long I keep at it.'

'There we are then. You're doing them anyway. Why not make a bit out of it and give others the pleasure of owning them?'

We went back to the sitting-room and he stood thinking for a few minutes. 'Tell you what! I'll provide you with pictures to enlarge and copy. Do them for me.'

I considered it, slightly dubious. 'Without permission, wouldn't I be infringing a copyright?'

'Not if the artist has been dead for at least fifty years, and as long as we show it as a reproduction. Forging the signature and trying to pass it off as the original is a different matter, but anything that goes out of my shop is

clean. You needn't worry. I'm on good terms with the
police.'

'All right. If you think the finished articles are worthy
of it.'

'Good,' he said. 'You know, this has all been most
interesting. What started as an unexpected dip in the
river has turned into a really entertaining afternoon.
Come over and see us some time, and I'd like Sally to
have a look at all this.'

He left me his address and telephone number, and I
saw him to his car. Then, with a wave of his hand, he
roared away.

I went indoors with a feeling of anti-climax, as if some
unexpected and exciting interlude had suddenly fizzled
out and left everything rather flat. I too had been
thoroughly entertained. I couldn't remember the last
time I'd enjoyed anybody's company so much. There was
something about him: a warmth plus a kind of controlled
recklessness. Our conversation had turned on many
things, and I had soon found out that he was fairly well
informed on all of them. I realized too that I had told him
a damn sight more about myself than I had got out of him.
But there was quite a lot I hadn't told him.

By most standards I'd had a reasonably lucky start in
life, for I had been born of wealthy parents, my mother in
her own right and my father as a director of a well-
established firm of biscuit manufacturers. As an only
child I was inclined to be spoilt at first, but this was soon
knocked out of me when I went to boarding-school.
However, once I had accepted and become used to the
discipline, my passage was reasonably smooth. I was fairly
popular because I was average, a good listener and a soft
touch if anybody became hard up at the end of the month.
I was hopeless at sports. I was strong enough but I had
no eye for a ball and my timing and physical and mental
co-ordination at anything athletic were way out. In this

respect I was regarded as something of a joke.

I did not go on to university because I didn't want to. I think my father was a little disappointed but he agreed that instead I should take a five-year course at the Architectural Association School of Architecture. There I did well enough to gain my diploma and qualify as an ARIBA and was taken into a firm of architects run by a friend of my father.

By the time I was thirty I had fallen violently in and out of love on several occasions. I wasn't naïve about sex but I could never acquire the same free-and-easy, love-'em-and-leave-'em attitude of most of my male friends and colleagues. Once some sort of relationship began, logic and reason abandoned me. I put the female concerned on a very high pedestal, thought that, as well as possessing all the virtues, she was extremely beautiful and could not understand why other men weren't intensely envious. Afterwards in retrospect I could see where I'd gone wrong, but I could not prevent it happening again.

Then I met Irene and our affair didn't fizzle out within a few months. In fact, after a year we were married. For a while things were fine but it couldn't last like that. Our tastes and inclinations were vastly different. I am interested in books, art and languages (I can now speak French, Italian and German fairly fluently), but I do not like pop music, dancing or cocktail-parties with the pointless gossipy conversation. I tried to conform and I believe she tried to meet me half-way, but it was no good. For ten years we struggled on, seeing less and less of each other, the strain mounting. We had no children, which grieved me, because she didn't want any.

Then I confirmed what I had suspected for some time. She was seeing somebody else. I taxed her with it, quietly but insistently, until she lost her temper. This caused me to shout to make myself heard and it ended with her crying and storming out of the house. I heard her Mini start up and then drive away on full throttle. I never saw her again. Ten minutes later she was killed in a car crash.

I had suffered two shocks in one. I was shattered. I felt guilty, illogically perhaps, but I couldn't help blaming myself. The thought kept going round and round in my head that if only I had tackled the matter differently, been less persistent, she would still be alive.

I found it difficult to face people. I lived within myself, wanting no one and avoiding everyone. Fortunately I had enough to live on, so I left my firm and retired into my shell.

Like most people, at times I look searchingly in the mirror, assessing the image others see. A few months later the face that stared back at me had changed considerably. There were more grey streaks in the thickish brown hair, round the eyes were lines that had not been there before and there were added lines too over the thick, straight brows and at each side of the mouth. I had also lost weight.

Physically I didn't feel bad but I realized that this couldn't go on. I decided. I severed all links with the past, searched for and found the haven in which I now live. Luckford is a delightful village. It has one main street with a pub, the Stag, a post-office and general store and rows of small terraced houses of some antiquity. There is a Norman church, a small hall, a pond and a green. My cottage is off a narrow lane leading from the main street and stands on a rise with a panoramic view of fields of corn and grass, and woods – a patchwork of colours as far as the eye can see. Two hundred yards away is the river.

It wasn't long before I felt better and looked better. After a cautious start on their part, I had been accepted by the regulars in the Stag. I enjoyed the lunch-time or odd evening visit there and gradually content replaced despair. I was living again.

In living again I began to miss the warmer companionship of close friends, but I still rejected the idea of going back into the past.

Then Hannaford came into my life.

A few days went by. I wanted to see him again but I decided that it wouldn't be in good taste to follow up his invitation too soon.

As it turned out, he rang me first. We had parted on christian name terms and as soon as I announced my number he said, 'John! This is Tom Hannaford. Will you be in this afternoon?'

'Hallo!' I said, enthusiasm coming automatically into my voice. 'This afternoon? Yes, I can be.'

'Will it be all right if I bring Sally over?'

'Sure. Fine. I'll look forward to it. What time?'

'About three be all right?'

'When you like. Did you tell her about rescuing me from a watery grave?'

He lowered his voice. 'No. I said I'd fallen in and you'd been near by and lent me the change of clothes.'

'Why? I'd want to boast about it.'

'Remember your promise! She might tell somebody else and then the press could get hold of it. Leave it that way. See you about three.'

Mrs Simmonds, a widow from the village who came in four times a week to clean up for me, hadn't been gone long, but I still gave the place the once-over and shifted things round a bit, which wasn't like me. I'm not normally over-conscious about impressing anybody about anything.

I started to speculate on Mrs Hannaford. How old would she be and what would she be like? I've known some surprising partnerships: handsome, athletic men married to quite insignificant women, and sometimes really stunning females teamed up with gawky, colourless clots. I hoped I wasn't going to be disappointed in this case, although why it should have mattered to me, God knows!

When they arrived I found myself looking at her with a sense of relief. She was of middle height for a woman, slim, dark and elegant. They went well together.

I ushered them in and Hannaford introduced us. After that, mainly because of him, there wasn't a moment's awkwardness. She thanked me for my hospitality to her husband and for lending him my clothes, which they had brought back cleaned and pressed. They stayed for a couple of hours and left with a promise from me that I would visit them. A firm date was agreed for the following Friday.

When the day arrived, I cleaned up my Triumph Estate so that it looked fairly respectable and drove to Bulford, a small town I had passed through on a number of occasions. Hannaford had given me adequate and clear directions and I didn't have any trouble finding their house.

It was on the outskirts, among several other well-spaced properties, and I must say I was impressed. White ranch fencing divided their ground from the highway and a smooth lawn sloped gradually up to the building, a stone, brick and wood chalet with a steep gabled roof of green interlocking tiles. There was a wide drive-in to a flat-roofed garage and a parking space for several cars.

As I got out of my car Hannaford came down the stone steps from the porch. With that lazy, confident air of his, he looked like an advertisement for men's wear in one of the glossies: fawn lightweight jacket and slacks – jacket open and one hand in pocket – brown silk shirt and dull gold cravat.

'No bother finding us, then?'

'None whatever. In fact, anticipating that there might be, I'm a bit early, I think.'

'Never! Come on in.'

He ushered me through a large square hall into a comfortable sitting-room and Sally turned from the

window and came forward. Before, I'd considered her
attractive and a fitting partner for Hannaford as I judged
him. Now, she looked positively ravishing. A long, sleeveless turquoise dress allowed just the hint of a cleavage, slid
in at the waist and tightened over her hips to accentuate
her excellent figure.

I was holding her hand and she was smiling. How white
her teeth were! Her near-bronze hair, long and shining!
Her eyes, green and mysterious! I felt suddenly like a
bumbling clodhopper with large feet.

'Hallo, Mr Bryant.'

I know I gave a slight bow and thought to myself,
What the hell's the matter with you? Pull yourself
together, man! You weren't like this before.

Hannaford came to my rescue. 'Come on, you two,
dispense with the formality. It should be Sally, John and
Tom. Now, drinks first. Sherry? How do you like it,
John?'

'Medium dry?'

'Medium dry it is.'

Sally and I grinned at each other as if agreeing on
something about Hannaford, and in no time it all became
friendly and intimate. I was still very conscious of her
and hoped it didn't show too much. As the evening pro-
gressed through an excellent meal to coffee and more
drinks back in the sitting-room, my inhibitions faded and
my tongue loosened. I have read a lot and have my own
pet theories on several contentious subjects which I
usually keep to myself, but Hannaford coaxed them out of
me, enlarged on them and contributed more or less
parallel ones of his own. Sally listened most of the time,
chipping in with the odd question now and again. Time
sped by.

As I was about to leave I said, 'Sally, before I met you
I was hoping you would be like you are – just right for
Tom,' and it was only on reflection that I remembered

their exchanging glances and laughing a little less spontaneously than before.

On my way out we passed a very good Fragonard reproduction in the hall, a young girl of the period in profile, and, as I stopped for a second to admire it, Hannaford said, 'D'you think you could do that?'

It was fine stuff but the line was clear and delicate and I was fairly good at that. Matching the colours, I thought, shouldn't be too difficult. When I didn't answer immediately he took it down from the wall.

'Here! I'll put it in your car. See what you can do.'

'I don't know. Won't you miss it?'

'I'll hang something else up for the time being.'

'I'll have a go then,' I said.

Hannaford and I shook hands and Sally surprised me by kissing me on the cheek.

CHAPTER II

I took nearly a week over the portrait. Hannaford called in once to see how it was going and studied it from different angles without comment. Finally he went round and looked at the back.

'Yours is on canvas,' I said, 'but I'm using delterboard.'

'So I see.'

'Canvas is difficult to stretch to get it just right and this is already primed.'

He nodded as if he fully understood and approved.

'It seems to be coming on well,' he said. 'See you in a few days.' He was off, he said, on his travels round the country in search of antiques.

I got quite a kick out of copying the Fragonard and, as I was doing it for Hannaford, I put more into it than I

would have done otherwise. Those few days passed
pleasantly.

I had not forgotten the effect Sally had had on me,
but I put it down to lack of practice, as it were. For nearly
two years women had been creatures to avoid, and I had
not been ready to meet someone like her on such a friendly
basis.

In between my work on the Fragonard, I read, watched
television and went for walks. I also kept up my sessions
at the Stag, where it gradually became apparent that I was
being treated with less reserve by the regulars there. I
had already been accepted but, although their attitude
towards me had been by no means unfriendly, it had struck
me that they regarded me as a sort of headmaster. Perhaps
it was my habit of years to think a great deal before I
ventured any comment on a subject under discussion and,
as I had usually researched into things a great deal more
than they had, I was able to come up occasionally with
facts which were relevant and indisputable. I had, I
imagine, become a 'character' to them.

George Slater, the landlord, a large and phlegmatic ex-
policeman, always welcomed me most cordially. I stood
my drinks and accepted the return, but as far as the others
were concerned I suppose I hadn't given away much of
myself.

At least I hadn't until after I became friendly with
Hannaford. We speak not only with our mouths. There is a
silent communication that is meaningful to others, even if
they don't immediately understand it. It comes over at
three times the speed of light, creating impressions which
take a lot to remove. Anyway, some change must have
come over me because now a warmth was added to the
perhaps undeserved respect shown to me.

Tony Sopwith, a large, rugger-type who travelled in
pharmaceutical goods, started the ball rolling by pulling

my leg for the first time there and setting the mood. I enjoyed it all and, I thought, gave back as good as I got.

As I was leaving, Sopwith called out, 'John, you've got hidden depths. I bet it's a woman that's brought you out!'

'Maybe,' I said, 'and maybe not,' and we all laughed.

The portrait sat there finished for five days before Hannaford called. Mrs Simmonds, having sweated on her beloved floors, flicked it unnecessarily with a duster. 'My, that's nice,' she said.

Hannaford, when he came, stared at it and then said, 'By God, you're a genius! It's a bloody sight better than mine.'

'Genius be damned. But I'm quite pleased with it. Some of the colours are a fraction of a shade out. I wouldn't want to compare it with the original.'

'I certainly think it's too good to sit here doing nothing.'

'Okay. You can have it.'

'Business. I'll sell it for you.'

'I don't like conducting business between friends. I did it for you. Take it.'

'Captain,' he said, 'you're talking utter bilge, which is unlike you. How can I ask you to do another if that's your attitude?'

'Just ask.'

'Oh no. If this is a sample, I'd like some more and I wouldn't dream of asking you unless you agree to take your cut.'

I considered it. 'All right, if it means that much to you.'

'It does. You'll see.'

He stayed for a couple of hours, and as always when with him, time passed very quickly. When he left he placed the two portraits carefully in the back of his car, and I stood on the drive beside him as he started up. The engine roared into life and after the initial burst he let it tick over quietly and turned his head.

'Can you call at the shop the day after tomorrow?'

'Sure. What time?'

'After three. I'll be there by then.'

'Right. I'm interested. How's Sally, by the way?'

'Fine. She sends her regards.'

'Give her mine,' I said.

I found a convenient parking place, walked back to the shop and stood on the pavement sizing it up. A sign in Gothic lettering across the top had the words ANTIQUES AND REPRODUCTIONS. Previously on my occasional visits to Northminster I had only flashed by, but I now saw that it was no ordinary antique shop. Square panes glistened in large bow windows each side of the entrance and black and white paint gleamed on the woodwork. Inside, everything was most invitingly displayed. On the right at the back I could see a book section, shelf upon shelf.

I went in. A man of about fifty, short by my standards, dressed in clerical grey, came up to me as I stood there. He regarded me in a scholarly manner with a pair of friendly, intelligent, blue eyes.

'Good afternoon, sir. Is there anything in particular you are looking for?'

'I expected to see Mr Hannaford,' I said.

'Oh, you're Mr Bryant! He's here. I'll get him.'

He went through a door at the back and returned, trailing behind Hannaford.

'I should have been looking out for you, John. This is Clive Chapman, my manager. He *is* the business, really.'

I shook hands with Chapman, who said, 'I think there's more than a slight exaggeration there, Mr Bryant.'

'Come over here, John,' said Hannaford. I followed him deep into the shop and there, on a wall among landscapes and seascapes, was the girl I had painted. It was nicely framed and a small notice was attached to it: 'Sold.'

Hannaford produced a buff envelope and gave it to me.

'Sixty pounds there! I sold it yesterday only two hours after we'd stuck it in the window. I got ninety.'

I was amazed. 'Ninety pounds!'

'Sure thing. See what I mean about wasting your talents?'

'I'm no business man,' I said. 'I'm not cut out for it. Frankly I don't need the money. You can give what you think I should take to any charity you like. I was pleased to do it for you and delighted that someone feels it worth buying.'

At first he frowned. Then he put his head on one side and eyed me shrewdly.

'You're an odd cove! I'm certainly not giving it to charity for some organizer to get his sticky fingers on. You do what you like with it and any more you get, but my advice is to stick it in an old sock under the floorboards, or spend it.'

That seemed to settle the matter, and I did feel a slight lift that the portrait had been sold so quickly and for such a good price.

He showed me over the shop, explaining the merits of various items and what they were likely to fetch, and I browsed among the books, coming away with a very nice copy of Thoreau's *Walden* which he wouldn't let me pay for.

During the next few months I saw a great deal of Hanna-ford. Except for periods when he was out of the district he called regularly, at least twice a week. I looked forward to his visits and came to depend on them. I completed two other paintings for him, but he never pressed me about them and it was obvious that our growing friendship had nothing to do with the business side of our relationship.

Christmas came and we exchanged cards, but I didn't see him during the season as they went away. Then spring arrived, by which time I had completed another reproduction.

I called only once at his home, for lunch. I hadn't seen Sally since that first evening and, whether it was because I had schooled myself against it or because some vital spark had gone from her, she didn't have quite the same effect on me.

However, a few weeks later when we all went on a picnic together, I was made to realize that it was still there. On this occasion we were accompanied by another couple, a man named Statham and his rather insipid wife. Statham was a robust extrovert who immediately tried to outgrip me when we shook hands. He was something on the Stock Exchange. His wife said very little. I noticed that a certain unspoken intimacy seemed to exist between Statham and Sally and I realized that it caused me more than a twinge of jealousy. I knew it was stupid but I couldn't do a thing about it. The occasion would have been a dead loss if it hadn't been for Hannaford, who somehow steered each of us to reasonable relaxation.

Almost exactly a year after our first meeting, Hannaford put a proposition to me that, with all I owed him, I couldn't refuse. He had telephoned in the morning to say that he would like to see me and added, 'Does your woman come in today?'

I said that she did.

'What time does she leave?'

'About twelve.'

'Anybody else likely to come in the afternoon?'

'Shouldn't think so. Why?'

'I have something rather confidential to impart.'

'What about?'

'Come on, Captain, not on the phone! See you about two?'

'Okay by me. But you've left me in the air and very curious.'

'Sorry about that, but unavoidable as you'll find out.'

On and off during the morning I speculated and had a slight feeling of apprehension that it was something to do with one of the portraits I'd let him have. Had there been some legal slip-up?

When Mrs Simmonds left I went down to the Stag for an hour, where I joined in a discussion with Harry Thread-gold, Reg Smailes and George behind the bar on the growing tendency towards violence and what could be done about it. I had a snack there too, so that by the time I got home there was nothing to do except wait and continue to wonder.

At two-fifteen came his signal, two sharp stabs on the doorbell. As soon as he came in, he said, 'Could do with a coffee if you've got some lurking around.'

I knew he liked it black without sugar, so I didn't have to ask him.

'Come out in the kitchen and start telling me what this is all about.'

'Wait until the coffee's ready.' He settled in an arm-chair. 'Is the back door locked?'

I had put the kettle on and I went to the door.

'You want it locked?' I called out.

'If you don't mind. Can't have anybody creeping up on us.'

I locked it, more baffled than ever, and when I took the coffee in I saw that he'd shut the window.

'Sorry about the cloak and dagger,' he said, 'but I don't believe in taking unnecessary risks.'

We sat opposite each other for a few moments, he sipping his coffee and I wondering what the hell he was going to come out with. Then he put his cup down. 'John, I'd like your help. If you don't want to give it, okay. I'll understand. In fact I've hesitated to ask you in case you still feel unnecessarily indebted.'

'I've already told you. Anything within my capabilities.'

'Rather a sweeping offer, that. You wait a minute. You'll have to take a lot on trust. I don't want to involve you more than necessary.'

'For God's sake, Tom, cut the preface and get to the first chapter.'

This seemed to amuse him for he grinned and nodded. 'An apt turn of phrase! I am going to tell you about a man named Clarence Cunningham, one-time Guards Officer who should have been cashiered but was saved that ignominy by an astute lawyer and some outside influence. Now over the past six months to my knowledge he's swindled at least three people out of thousands, including two elderly women who've lost most of their life savings.'

He finished his coffee and I said, 'How?'

'He runs a semi-legitimate estate business in Handsworth, Birmingham, with a partner named Swift. We can forget Swift, as he doesn't come into it any more. The other side of the business he keeps mainly to himself. It concerns property in Spain and the people he deals with are conned by an apparently attractive scheme and his persuasive manner. They hand over their money, sign contracts without fully understanding them and when time goes by and their dreams of a villa in the sun don't materialize, it's too late. He's done them, but legally. Spain has the advantage of being a long way away and he trades on the hopes and gullibility of people who could not normally afford anything like the sort of thing he appears to offer. After a lapse of time he sells the land he's acquired

to someone else, and then buys a few other cheap plots and
starts all over again.

'How do you know all this?'

'I told you you'd have to take me on trust.'

He let this sink in and I said, 'More coffee?'

'No, thanks. Now, I want you to help me to teach Mr
Cunningham a sharp lesson. I want you to answer an
advertisement he's put in the paper, showing interest in
his scheme. Then I want you to arrange to see him.'

'You want me to go to his office?'

'No.'

'You want him to come here?'

'Not here either. I am renting a house in Marchester,
seventy miles from here. Letters to him will be from there,
and the signature, yours, will be copied by me so that
afterwards you can honestly say you didn't write them or
send them. Anyway, he will assume this house is yours and
that's where he will call to see you.'

So far it didn't make much sense to me. 'Why can't I
meet him here and sign the letters myself?'

'Because I don't want you to get involved afterwards.
I did say, Captain, that you'd have to take so much on
trust. I know what I'm doing.'

I had to concede him that probability.

'Okay. So, for his benefit I'm the resident of this house
in Marchester. What then?'

'Not only the resident but the owner. When he arrives
you give him the impression that you are more than a little
interested in his scheme, that you are looking ahead and,
with taxes and inflation, you don't think you can afford
to keep the place much longer. Furthermore you're
looking for a worthwhile investment. D'you think you
can do that?'

'I don't know until I try. I've never considered myself
a potential Olivier.'

'Maybe not, but for this job you're just the right type.

Honest and trusting, and you look it. Having convinced you of the infallibility of his scheme, he will be hoping for some tangible evidence of your intentions in the form of your cash and a signature on a contract. Here you must hedge a bit without diminishing your apparent enthusiasm. Say you've got to get the money out of a building society and ask for a few days' grace. Suggest that he leaves the contract and that you will sign it and send it on with the amount agreed upon. He'll probably express doubt that he could hold on to any specific property without some guarantee, so you offer to give him a cheque for a hundred pounds as a deposit if he will reserve the plot you fancy for a week.'

'You want me to give him a hundred quid?'

'Not so bloody likely. Let me sign one of your cheques beforehand and leave the stub blank. You can make out you're filling it in and signing it. Then as soon as he's gone telephone your bank and cancel it.'

'I thought you said you didn't want me to get involved afterwards. If I ring the bank I shall be.'

'You pick up the phone and speak to somebody at the bank. How can they prove it's you? Tell them you are staying at Marchester for a few weeks. They will ask for confirmation by letter and they will get one from me in your name. They won't query it after that. The signature will be good enough and the number on the cheque will prove it's you. People who pinch cheques don't cancel them!'

I rubbed my forehead to emphasize my confusion.

'This is all getting damned complicated. My head's going round and round.'

He chuckled. 'Sorry about that. I suppose it is.'

'Why bother about a cheque? Can't I just say I'll let him know and get rid of him?'

'You could, but it wouldn't fit in with my plans. I want him to leave feeling reasonably satisfied that he's nailed another sucker. Your cheque in his pocket will confirm this impression. No one parts with a ton unless he means business.' His face straightened into more serious lines. 'I've thought of everything, including the unexpected. If you do what I ask, without worrying, you'll be helping to put the skids under a right bastard the law can't touch.'

I agreed of course, but I couldn't really see any point in it all.

'You reckon that this will teach him a lesson?'

'There's a bit more to it, as I've said.'

'There is one thing that troubles me. I don't know what this character is like and I don't know what you're going to do. He'll have seen me and he'll know that I am John Bryant. Suppose he finds out eventually that I live here and starts pestering?'

'Why should he do that?'

'I don't know. As I said, I don't know what you're up to.'

'Look, Captain, can't you trust me? Later I'll write to him in your name, telling him you've had second thoughts and have decided to leave it for the time being, that you've cancelled your cheque and will be in touch with him if you change your mind. If by some fluke he does meet you again, let me know. He won't trouble you after that.'

With this cryptic remark I had to be satisfied. Of course if I had been my normal, pre-Hannaford self I wouldn't have dreamed of getting involved in such a tortuous scheme. But he *had* saved my life. I had grown to like him tremendously. And not only *like* him. There was that about him, some magical influence that seemed to raise the quality of living, an unflamboyant magnetism which, now I can think about it objectively, must have smothered reasonable doubts and common sense. Also – and this is only a supposition – perhaps I was subconsciously fed up with my own cautious and somewhat introverted nature. I was going to believe what I wanted to believe, and why he was bothering about somebody else's misdeeds hardly mattered.

'When d'you want this to happen?' I asked.

He drew from his pocket an addressed envelope from which he took a letter. This he handed to me. The letter-heading was printed, The Beeches, Long Lane, Marchester, and there was a telephone number. The rest was type-written, dated the following day, and requesting from Mr Cunningham further details as advertised. There was a space for signature and under that 'John Bryant' in type.

'If you let me have a sheet of paper and a specimen of your signature, I'll do the rest.'

I went to my desk, pulled out a pad and scrawled my signature at the top. Like most signatures it doesn't bear much resemblance to my name and it was, I should say, difficult to copy with the easy flourish which is the mark of the original. However, after studying it for a few moments, he filled the page with his efforts and finally it was almost perfect. When he had signed the letter it would have fooled me.

'Now, John, you can back out if you want to and I'll think none the worse of you for it.'

'I'm not going to back out. You know that.'

He put the letter in the envelope and sealed it.

'I'll post this tomorrow,' he said.

After he had gone I sat thinking, and gradually an agreeable excitement began to replace any misgivings I might have had. I had always been the least adventurous of mortals and the prospect ahead, although apparently devoid of risk as far as I was concerned, would at least be intriguing. I should be engaging in a conspiracy with apparently laudable motives and taking an active if sheltered part in whatever mysterious scheme Hannaford had in mind.

So when three days later Hannaford called with a

letter from Mr Cunningham, I was fully in tune with the idea. Mr Cunningham had replied on good quality paper, neatly headed 'Overseas Properties Ltd', showing the registered office address and giving the directors as C. J. Cunningham and F. E. Swift. He said that they had several desirable properties for sale in Spain, some in course of erection, and he would be delighted to call and see me and place his expert advice at my disposal on Tuesday, Wednesday or Thursday of the following week when he would be in my area. Would I please complete the form enclosed and state which day and what time would be suitable? If none of them was convenient, I was to give some dates when I should be available. Also enclosed was a brochure giving a colourful account, with pictures, of the proposed area and the properties, glamourizing the advantages of the scheme they had in mind.

Hannaford filled in the form, somewhat exaggerating my potential prospects as a fairly affluent but naïve client, and it was agreed that he should write back saying that Tuesday at about twelve noon would suit me very nicely.

I turned over the pages of the brochure and Hannaford chuckled.

'You've got to hand it to him. It's clever, very clever. How d'you feel about things now?'

'I'm game,' I said. 'If that's all you want me to do?'

'Well . . . it is and it isn't. Let's say I want your interview to follow a pattern. I'll explain when we get to the house on Tuesday.'

'What's the matter with now?'

'Because we're not there now. I'll be here about seven, leave my car and you can drive us both over in yours. Then you'll understand.'

When Tuesday came, I awoke alert and almost eager for the fray. Hannaford had filled in a few further details of some of Cunningham's activities and I must say the man sounded a most insidious scoundrel. I still had no notion what Hannaford had in mind, but I felt sure he wasn't going to all this trouble unless it was something that would really hurt.

He arrived on time and put his car in my garage before we drove off. About nine we stopped for breakfast at a small place just outside Marchester, and then he directed me to Long Lane and The Beeches.

It was a large Victorian house, with a modern extension, practically hidden from the lane by high, neatly-trimmed privet. There was a wide, curved in-and-out drive and a large garage at one end.

The first thing Hannaford did was to get me to put the car in the garage. Then he shut the doors and I followed him to the main porch.

'You've rented this for a month,' he said, as he put the key in the heavy door and opened it.

'It must have cost me!' I said.

'A small outlay, considering. I'll show you the main room where I want you to take him, and tell you a few things. Then you'd better familiarize yourself with the layout in case he wants to go to the loo.'

The room was at the back of the house. It was spacious, with a high ceiling, and furnished, if not to my taste, comfortably enough. A good quality blue carpet, which had seen better days, covered the floor except for an edging of dark polished boards. One of these creaked as I went in. There were several heavy leather armchairs, some with frayed cord piping, a rather nice oak coffee table and a huge brick fireplace with a pseudo-log electric fire stuck in the middle of it. Heavy blue curtains hung at the windows. Against one wall was a desk, a thickly-carved upright chair and, near that, a bar set-up with a mirror back and a rather scratched oak surface.

I looked at the bottles and glasses and said, 'Well, that's a welcome sight anyway.'

'Not until this is all over, please. I want you to keep a clear head. Will you promise me you won't touch a drop until I say so?'

'Okay. I wasn't thinking of just yet anyway.'

'Not until I say so?'

'I promise.'

'Now,' he said, 'this is what I want you to do. When he comes, ask him in here and sit him over there.' He pointed to a chair some way from the desk. 'Listen to his proposition and sound a bit cautious at first. You can let it drop that, with taxation as it is, you don't think you can afford to keep up this place. Spin things out a bit, ask questions and eventually agree to give him the cheque for a hundred pounds. Go to the desk where you'll have your back to him.' I followed him over to the desk. 'Make out you're writing a cheque and give him this one I've signed.'

'Seems simple enough.'

'Now I'll sit over here where he'll be sitting and you go through the motions.'

I did as he said.

'That's fine. You're just the right width! I couldn't see what you were doing. There is one more thing.' He led me to the bar. 'Here are two bottles, gin and whisky, and also a few tonics. When you've given him the cheque, ask him if he'd like a drink to seal the bargain. He'll almost certainly say he wants a gin and tonic. It might be whisky, but I doubt it. Pour him a drink and one for yourself, but you'll have tonic only.'

'Why can't I have a whisky?'

He looked at me sorrowfully. 'I thought you wanted to help?'

'I do.'

'Right then. On *no* account have anything except tonic. Okay?'

I shrugged. 'Okay.'

'Now we come to your final act. As soon as he's finished his drink, look at your watch and, with apologies, tell him you must ask him to leave as you have to pick up somebody from the station. You'd forgotten about this when you made the appointment with him. Having got your cheque, he won't hang about. The rest you leave to me. And no drinks, remember! You'll have to drive shortly after and you could come unstuck, which would ruin everything.'

'So that's why you don't want me to have a drink. But I'd be all right.'

'Not if somebody ran into you and a bobby asked you to blow into a bag. We can't chance it.'

'Where will you be?'

'I'll be close handy. Now, have a look round and feel you own the place . . . sir!'

Mr Cunningham arrived almost on the dot, which gave me the idea that he'd probably scouted the area earlier and so knew exactly where to go. The house wasn't all that easy to find.

He parked his shiny blue Audi on the drive, and from behind the curtains in a front room I watched his tall, military figure, brown briefcase under his arm, stroll unhurriedly to the front porch. The bell rang and I opened the door. There he was, smartly dressed in grey worsted, thinning fair hair, pale blue eyes set in genial lines, a crisp moustache and an expression of sincere goodwill.

'Mr Bryant?' he asked.

'Yes. It's Mr Cunningham, is it?'

'That's right. I always make a point of being as punctual as possible.'

I ushered him in and led him to the room chosen.

'I say,' he said, looking round with open admiration, 'I like this. Dignity here and old world charm.' He nodded several times and then, as if suddenly remembering why he'd come, brought himself back to the matter of business and unzipped his case.

I offered him *the* chair and sat down near him.

'What do you think so far?' he said. 'I ask this because we don't like to pressurize people. Sales gimmicks are out. We don't need them. The scheme sells itself.'

Following Hannaford's instructions, I wasn't going to appear too easy to handle. 'It hasn't completely sold itself to me yet. There are one or two things.'

'That's what I'm here for.'

'How is it that your firm is able to offer such advantageous terms? I hope you don't mind my asking, only . . .'

He raised his hand. 'Not at all. A good question and I was going to explain anyway. Most builders of property operate on credit. That is, they borrow money on interest and take this into account when calculating their profit margin. If there are no unreasonable hold-ups during erection they sell within a month or two and don't do so badly. However, if through bad weather, strikes or a difficult market there is a considerable delay in completing and selling the property, then they can be in trouble. And believe me, it happens. All the time they have to keep paying interest and I have known cases where the banks have had to take over and the builders have gone bankrupt.'

I nodded understandingly.

'Bearing all this in mind, you will realize how different it is if a builder doesn't have to rely on banks, pays no interest and isn't unduly hustled for time – although of course he wants to finish as soon as possible to get his money – and knows that the house will be sold as soon as it is completed.'

I nodded again and said, 'I can see that. But why can't they do that in this country?'

'Ah!' He laughed and shook his head as if I had raised

a sore point. 'You may indeed ask. The reason quite plainly is that people won't do it. A villa in Spain, a place to go to for a holiday, an investment for the future at a bargain price, that's the difference! I tell you, Mr Bryant, we have no difficulty in getting investors for this. But we are choosey who we have. That's why we asked you to fill in a form and why I've called here instead of asking you to visit our office.'

'Choosey?'

He took from his case two large, folded, parchment-like sheets. One showed plans of different types of residence, all very attractive, and photographs of completed properties. The other was more or less a map showing plots of land, all numbered.

'In fairness to other occupiers, we like to feel that the neighbours they have won't cause any friction. We try to fit type to type, as it were. For instance – ' he pointed to a plot numbered 5 – 'Stranevski, the concert pianist, has this one. And here – ' his finger slid across to No. 9 – 'Rosswell, the author, has this one.' I'd never heard of either of them! 'Theirs are nearly completed. We try to avoid taking on people who are likely to be brash or difficult socially. It hasn't taken me long to realize that you are a most suitable applicant in this respect.'

I assumed an expression of mild doubt and he caught on.

'Don't get me wrong. It's just a case of choosing reasonable people. You can do what you like there but it's a question of standards. I don't suppose you'd want a convicted bank robber or a swindler living next door to you.'

The irony of this remark made my lip twitch slightly.

'I get your point,' I said. 'What are the other terms?'

'Properties 3, 4, 6 and 8 are still on offer. As you can see, the view is excellent. One thousand starts the building, a further thousand when the roof is on and two thousand on completion. The place will be fully furnished and you can occupy it for two months each year for three years and then you will have sole possession. During the rest of the three years it is leased for holidays and we share the rent. If you care to start off with two thousand, the property becomes wholly yours within two years.'

On the face of it, it seemed an attractive investment.

'It sounds good,' I said. 'I'd like to think it over.'

'Of course you would, but unfortunately I can't guarantee that the plots we've offered will still be available. That's a risk you'll have to take. The last thing I want to do is to rush you into anything, but I have to point this out.'

I stood up and walked about with an expression of deep concentration. I picked up the contract again and then the plans and studied them.

'I like it. I like it,' I said. 'And I rather fancy plot 4. If I were to give you a cheque for a hundred pounds could you reserve it for me for, say, a week, while I transfer some money from my building society?'

He made a show of thinking heavily about it and then doing me a favour.

'All right,' he said. 'I'll give you a week.'

'I'll opt for the two thousand plan and send it to you with the contract. This place is getting too much for me, what with taxes and everything.'

For a moment it seemed that he might try and press for a signature on the contract as well, and then his face cleared as if he'd thought better of it.

'Fine,' he said. 'I'm sure you won't regret it.'

I went over to the desk and performed my act. When I took over to him the cheque Hannaford had signed, he gave me a receipt.

'Most inhospitable of me!' I said. 'Before you leave, you must join me in a drink.' I got up and went to the bar. 'What'll it be?'

'Gin and tonic?'

'Yes.' I poured the gin, turned and, letting him gauge the tonic, stopped at his signal. I gave him the glass and then, with my back to him, poured myself a tonic.

As I sat down again, he raised his glass. 'Thanks and cheers!' he said. 'So you're thinking of selling this place?'

'I'll have to sooner or later. There's only me now and it's rather big. Mind you, I'll miss it.' I had warmed to my task and thought I was doing rather well.

'Any idea how much it'll fetch?'

'Frankly, no. When I've made up my mind, I'll get a valuation.'

He didn't probe any further and, not surprisingly, didn't offer to negotiate for me.

I saw him tilt his glass for the last time and looked at my watch.

'It's rather later than I thought,' I said. 'Will you excuse me if I ask you to leave? When I made this arrangement with you, I'd quite forgotten that I have to pick somebody up from the station.'

'Of course,' he said and stood up immediately, holding out his hand. 'I look forward to hearing from you again. If you have any queries, just drop me a line. Once your plot has been secured, I'll let you know from time to time how things are progressing.'

I accompanied him to the door and said, 'It seems hardly the thing to push you off like this. I do apologize.'

'Not at all, Mr Bryant, not at all.' He gave a wave and walked to his car.

From a window I watched him get in and start up, drive a few yards and stop. Then he got out and stared at the front tyre nearest the house. I noticed that it was flat.

Hannaford's voice behind me said, 'Keep out of sight. You did marvellously. Now go into a back room and stay there, will you?'

I felt I was being cheated by being left out of whatever was going to happen now, and he sensed my unspoken resentment.

'Please, John! I've got to move fast and you're holding me up. Stay back there until I contact you. You've helped tremendously but I won't have you further involved.'

I went into the back room and shut the door, but I stayed close to it and listened. It seemed that the front door opened. Minutes passed before someone came into the hall. I heard dialling on the phone and then Hannaford's voice, 'Ambulance, please!' A few seconds later, 'Mr Bryant here, The Beeches, Long Lane, Marchester. Yes, Bryant. A man has collapsed on the driveway outside my house. He was apparently changing the wheel of his car. Yes, he's unconscious, or he was. Right. Thank you.'

I thought, My God, what *have* I let myself into? Suppose the man dies! There was no temptation to rush out and see. I wanted to hide somewhere. The flat tyre and the need for an ambulance? That was no accident. Hannaford had contrived it for his obscure purpose.

I was still trying to puzzle it out when I heard the sound of a vehicle and distant voices. Then the vehicle again, driving away. The front door shut and the door of the room I was in opened.

'We've done it, John! It worked to the letter.' Even in his enthusiasm he was still essentially calm. 'You heard? I can see you're worried.'

'Of course I am. I didn't expect him to be taken to hospital. Suppose he kicks the bucket?'

'He'll come to, a bit fuzzy, about half way to the hospital and he'll find a note from you saying he passed out while changing his wheel and that you're driving his car there and leaving it for him.'

'You're sure he'll be all right?'

'Quite sure. There was an otherwise harmless drug in

the gin you gave him. It's slow in action and almost impossible to trace without an autopsy – hence his flat tyre.'

'But . . .?'

'For your own good that's all you're going to know. Now get on to the bank and cancel that cheque, unless you want to lose a hundred! I'll be finishing off the wheel-changing part.'

'I can't remember the number,' I said.

He pulled out his wallet and handed me a slip of paper.

'I'd anticipated that. It's on there. And don't forget to tell them you are staying here.'

I telephoned the bank, gave my name and the number of the cheque and asked for it to be cancelled. They asked me for the reason and I said I'd changed my mind about something and agreed to confirm this in writing. I said I was staying at The Beeches for a few weeks.

By the time I'd finished Hannaford had completed his task and was putting the wheel with the deflated tyre in the back of Cunningham's car.

'I'll drive this,' he said, 'and you follow in yours. You can bring us both back here, and then we just wait.'

'I don't know what you're doing, but suppose he smells a rat when he comes to and decides to return here?'

'He won't smell anything. In perhaps a year or two he'll get a nasty shock, but by that time he won't remember enough to trace the cause.'

We were back within the hour and I hadn't said much during the return journey. Once inside he pulled out a newspaper cutting and gave it to me.

'So far you've taken me on trust, which I appreciate. Perhaps that'll make you feel better.'

It was an item from the *News of the World* of over a year ago. There was a photograph of an elderly, motherly type of woman, and the headlines read, WIDOW SWINDLED OUT OF LIFE'S SAVINGS. It went on to explain how a certain Rodney Marshall had persuaded her to invest in his scheme, how she had seen solicitors and had gone to the police who were powerless to help her, and how the paper's representative had eventually tracked down Marshall. They hadn't got anywhere with him either. His cover was foolproof. He had said little and subsequently went to ground. There was no doubt about the identity because Marshall's photograph was shown and it was clearly our Mr Cunningham.

'Satisfied?' asked Hannaford. 'Incidentally, neither Cunningham nor Marshall is his real name.'

'I believed you without this,' I said. 'But I'll still be relieved when I know he's all right.'

I had hardly said the words when the telephone rang.

'You answer it,' said Hannaford.

Cunningham's voice came over. 'Cunningham here, Mr Bryant. I'm just about to leave the hospital and I want to thank you for seeing I got there and for bringing my car. But I'm a bit mystified. What did happen?'

'You passed out while changing your wheel and I was worried in case you'd had a heart attack or a stroke. I didn't like the idea of moving you and you're no light weight, so I made you as comfortable as possible and sent for the ambulance.'

'That was good of you.'

'Not at all. What was the trouble?'

'No one seems to know. They checked my blood pressure and that was up a bit, but they couldn't find much else wrong with me. I feel all right now. They gave me some stuff to drink and some tablets, and told me to see my doctor. Thought I'd let you know in case you were worried about our deal.'

'I'm glad you did.'

'I'll be hearing from you, then?'

'In a few days. Glad you're okay now.'

'Thanks again.'

When I put the receiver down Hannaford, who had been listening at my ear, said, 'Perfect! Where's the contract?'

We went into the room which had been the scene of my brilliant dramatic performance. I retrieved the contract from the top of the writing desk. 'Here it is.'

'Have you read it?'

'In the circumstances I didn't bother. I made out I had.'

He took it, glanced down it and then pointed at a sub-paragraph in small, insignificant-looking print. 'Have a look at that.'

I read: 'Although every precaution will be taken to safeguard the investor's interest, no liability is accepted for delay in construction through industrial or political reasons, weather hazards or other unforeseen events.'

'Note the word "investor",' he said. 'As an "investor" you automatically accept some risk. Also the last three words, "other unforeseen events" just about cover everything. He can't go wrong. Your money would have gone straight into his pocket and you couldn't have proved a thing.'

'Why can't it be properly exposed?'

'It has been, but people soon forget.'

Now that I knew Cunningham was all right, I felt good again, and the newspaper cutting had removed any slight nagging sense of guilt I might have had.

'I wish you'd take me the whole way,' I said. 'What did you do?'

'Not on! We're leaving this place, and get this into your head. You've never been here. You've never heard of or seen Cunningham. You haven't written to him or signed any cheque for him. As far as you're concerned, he doesn't exist. Let's get back to your place and have that drink.'

My mood on the drive back was different from that on the way to Marchester for secretly I now felt a little proud of my performance and it gave me a lift. We were nearly home when Hannaford said, 'I'd like to take you up to Town for a really good evening out. When can you make it?'

'Most evenings,' I said.

'What about Thursday?'

'Suits me. Who's coming?'

He seemed to give this some thought. 'Sally might like a night out as well. All right by you?'

'Of course,' I said, and I couldn't quite keep the enthusiasm from my voice.

CHAPTER III

When Thursday came round I found myself pleasantly excited, and in acknowledging the reason, I accepted that as far as Sally was concerned there could be no future in it for me. My feelings were harmless enough because there was no possibility of my ever being tempted, and therefore I didn't feel guilty at the sensuous thrill I experienced when she was near me or when she looked at me and poured her personality over me.

I walked down to the local in the morning, had a couple of jars and a chat with the regulars, then a snack at home followed by twenty minutes' shut-eye.

At five I had a bath, put on a charcoal grey, light suit which I knew flattered my figure, a pale pink shirt and a cunningly-patterned silver-and-gold tie. I considered I was 'with it' without being showy. I ran my electric

razor over my face and rubbed in some after-shave.
Then I tried to read while I waited.

They were due at seven so I was a little surprised when
Hannaford arrived just after six.

'You're early,' I said and looked beyond him. 'Where's
Sally?'

'Change of plan. She can't make it after all. Got a
headache and doesn't fancy a late night.'

I tried not to let the disappointment show in my face.
He didn't seem over-concerned about her and I was on the
point of going into it more fully when I thought better of
it.

'Pity,' I said. 'What are we going to do, then?'

I guessed he had something in mind, otherwise he
would have rung me.

'You sound a bit deflated,' he said.

'No. No, far from it. It's just that I was geared up for
one thing this evening and have suddenly had to readjust
to something else.'

He looked at me with a tolerant, understanding
expression.

'John, my friend, if you don't mind my saying so that
attitude could be the bane of your life. Throw it over-
board. Slide along with things instead of bouncing off
them. You won't get damaged half as much.'

I grinned. 'I see you've brought your philosopher's
kit with you.'

'That's better. Now, if it's okay with you, we'll go
up to Town. Take about fifty minutes. To a club I belong
to. We're going to enjoy ourselves and it's on me. Unless
you want your handkerchief, keep your hands out of
your pockets.'

I wasn't quite sure what he had in mind but, as I'd
never failed to have an enjoyable time in his company,
I settled in the seat next to him and looked forward to a
pleasant evening.

He was a good driver. He had the knack of reading the
road a long way ahead, and he did it all with consummate
ease, chatting away between hazards, relaxed but very
much in command. As he was also a good car-handler,
which does not necessarily make a good driver, our pro-
gress was unaffected by jerks between gear changes or
swaying at corners or bends. I knew about these things
and could appreciate them, but I didn't have his natural
ability.

For about thirty minutes we talked of this and that,
covering a wide range of subjects, and it struck me then
that he always seemed to bring a refreshingly new angle
to established points of view. Whether I agreed with them
or not didn't matter, because unless your mind ran on
tramlines you couldn't dismiss his ideas out of hand.
Sometimes it seemed that he deliberately manufactured
contentious variations to bring fresh interest into conversation. If this were so, he certainly succeeded.

We hit a stretch of motorway and after a short period
when we drove along and said nothing, it struck me that
after all this time I still didn't know very much about
him. The thought exploded into words before I had time
to reflect that if he'd wanted me to know more he would
have told me.

'Tom,' I said, 'you're a remarkable person and you
baffle me. What makes you tick? What's your background?'

A wry grin creased his face. '"Remarkable" is an often
misapplied word. I believe it means strange, distinguished.
I don't think I'm that. Unusual? I suppose some people
could consider me unusual, but what is usual in one
decade is unusual in the next and vice versa. And what
is usual in one part of the world is unusual in another. As
for your being baffled, I think that ties up with what I've
already said. Our life styles have been different. We are

different in many ways. I hate being a prisoner of con-
vention, a slave to popular ideas. You, I think, have been
bound and gagged by them. Yet there is something in our
personalities which harmonizes. I have never known
anybody I have felt closer to or respected more, and if I
ever unwittingly caused you harm I should never forgive
myself. I think you have been stuck in a groove. Sorry for
the surfeit of metaphors, but here's the last one. Eat your
ice-cream before it melts!'

We were leaving the motorway and running into traffic
congestion which made further conversation difficult.
Hannaford's remarks had moved me but he still hadn't
told me much about himself.

We turned right at traffic lights, left, right and left
again and then drove on to a small private car park. We
got out and he locked the car.

'Through this alley,' he said, 'and round the corner.'

I followed him along the alley, which ran between two
buildings on one side of the car park, and then down some
stone steps. The words 'Canary Club' were stabbed out in
neon over a doorway which was open, and at the end of a
carpeted hall we came to a square shuttered panel and a
closed door. Hannaford pressed a bell button, the shutter
slid aside and a lantern-jawed male face appeared. A pair
of sharp, dark eyes stared at us and, on seeing Hannaford,
the wide, thin mouth stretched to one side.

'Evening, sir.' He shot me a quick glance as he fiddled
with something to his left. This must have released the
doorcatch, for there was a whirring noise and Hannaford
pushed the door open.

'Hallo, Sid,' said Hannaford. 'Things going well?'

Sid emerged from his cubby-hole and I reckoned he
could have stepped straight from the gaming tables of an
old-time Western. He was tall and thin, in a dark, tight-
fitting suit, the shoulders of the jacket sharply padded.

'Fair,' he said. 'Not so good as last night, but fair. Mr Warren won't be in till later. I told him you were coming.'

Hannaford nodded and led me towards swing doors and the muffled strains of rather treacly music. A long desk was on the right and a blonde in a very brief, yellow outfit gave us a smile. Then, as we passed through the doors, music and the hushed atmosphere of the place enveloped us. It was well patronized, and I looked across the scattered tables to a small stage where a dark, long-haired female with a willowy figure was just finishing her song. There was a burst of clapping – rather more dutiful than enthusiastic – and in no time at all people were chattering and clattering their knives and forks.

A sallow-faced waiter approached and it was obvious that Hannaford was well known to him. I was beginning to feel slightly irritated. The least Hannaford could have done, I thought, would have been to ask me if I wanted to go to a place like this. When he'd mentioned his club, I'd thought he meant some rather exclusive and dignified establishment. I'd no idea he went in for this type of thing. Furthermore, I didn't like being made to feel inferior, and the way everyone knew him and practically ignored me was a bit annoying.

Once again that knack he had of almost reading your thoughts showed itself. The menus had arrived, delivered by a curvaceous young woman scantily dressed in yellow. Her legs were encased in very thin, yellow stockings which disappeared round her crutch into fluffy, yellow stuff and above that, she was mostly bare flesh.

'I know what you're thinking,' he said. 'But do me and yourself a favour. Relax. This isn't what you expected, is it?'

'Frankly, no.'

'It's not costing you anything and I'll wager that if you let yourself go you'll have one hell of a time.'

Two large drinks had appeared on the table.

'Here's to a marvellous evening,' he said, 'and a long and happy friendship!'

I raised my glass and looked at the liquid inside. 'What is this?'

'A Canary Special. If you don't like it, we'll get your usual. Here's to you once again!'

What it had in it I don't know. It was mellow, the colour of light whisky. It wasn't sweet and it wasn't dry and it had a soothing effect. It seemed perfectly innocuous, but by the time I had drunk half of it I began to have my suspicions about that. However, I thought, I can take it, whatever it is.

The waitress reappeared, gave us a gorgeous smile and took our order. Hannaford asked me about wine and I said I'd leave it to him. I had another Canary Special while we waited, but I'm not so sure that *he* did. One thing, my feeling of resentment had vanished. I sat back and, given the slightest encouragement, I would have beamed happily at anybody who came within range.

A different female vocalist had taken the stage, all slinky, shimmering silver, and in a most seductive voice she threw everything into a soul-searching song of un-requited love. At the end I found myself still clapping enthusiastically when everyone else had stopped but, strange to say, didn't feel in the least embarrassed.

A few minutes later we were eating and drinking – wine now. I found myself being far more voluble than usual and enjoying it all. I dredged up some old philo-sophical theories I normally kept to myself, and Hannaford maintained a suitable balance between listening and commenting.

We were at the sweet course, the first bottle of wine nearly empty, when two young women seemed to come from nowhere. I was first aware that we had company when I saw a slim, naked midriff about two feet from me

and, allowing my eyes to travel slowly upwards, I took in
a flimsy, pink upper garment which skimmed across two
firm-looking breasts. She was gazing at me with large,
slightly almond-shaped eyes, and there was just the
suggestion of a smile. Allowing for my mellow condition,
I still think she was remarkably attractive, and I particularly liked the way her hair fell across part of her forehead, turned into a wave and spread neatly to the back of
her neck and shoulders. I beamed on her without hesitation, feeling like a big brother.

Hannaford was saying, 'Hallo! Hallo! This is a pleasant
surprise!'

Seeing him rise from his seat, I also stood up. The
young woman I had already smiled at came about up to
my chin and her companion, slightly older I should think,
was a little taller. I remember vaguely that she had a deep
blue outfit that would have raised a few eyebrows before
the permissive age burst upon us.

'Peggy, Frances, this is my very good friend John,'
said Hannaford, and I beamed again. Hannaford pulled
out a couple of chairs and I realized for the first time that
there were four at our table. 'Won't you join us? I insist!'

As they were already sliding into their seats before
he'd added the insisting part, the extra persuasion seemed
hardly necessary, but I assumed that as usual he knew what
he was doing.

Putting aside carnal influences, there is something
about a well-turned-out, good-looking woman which
enhances an occasion if you're in the right mood. I was
in such a mood.

Frances, the smaller of the two, had occupied a place
next to me, drinks appeared again as if by magic and I
lighted a cigarette for her. As Hannaford seemed to be
occupying the attention of Peggy, I felt free to engage
Frances whom, in an avuncular sort of way, I liked the
better of the two.

With an ease which was quite uncharacteristic, I heard myself saying, 'As Tom said, this is indeed a pleasant surprise. Do you know him well?'

'Well enough,' she said. Her voice was pleasant and accent-free. 'How long have you known him?'

I found the effort of working this out rather demanding and I gave up. 'A long time. Yes, a long time.'

Someone started to sing again, a man who produced extraordinary-sounding words I'd never heard before and who threw himself about in a remarkable fashion. I became fascinated by the curious effect the young man's hoarse rantings had on a section of the audience, particularly the younger women. He appeared to have a hypnotic influence over them and the louder he shouted the more it seemed to get inside them, causing them to shriek and cry out alarmingly. As he finished there was a tremendous burst of applause.

I whispered to Hannaford, 'D'you like that sort of stuff?'

'Not exactly, but it brings them in. Something for everybody is the aim here.' He topped up my glass from the bottle on the table.

I caught Frances looking at me rather covertly and when the dancing started again and Hannaford escorted Peggy to the floor, it seemed only right that we should follow suit.

I'm no gigolo but I've got a reasonable sense of balance and rhythm and there wasn't much room for intricate steps anyway. Feeling her close to me, warm and soft, and breathing in the scent she was wearing, the avuncular feeling began to wane and the fact that I must have been at least fifteen years older didn't seem to matter. There was a distinct stirring in my loins. She pressed herself very close to me as we swayed to the music and I suddenly felt, what the hell! Does it matter?

I also recalled Hannaford's words, 'Let yourself go

and you'll have the time of your life.' How had he known
that? He was incredible. I looked up to see where he was
and then noticed Peggy sitting at our table by herself.
With mild surprise I shifted my gaze and just caught
Hannaford going through a door with a small man in a dark
suit. Then we danced on and seemed to become wedged
in a cluster of smooching bodies at the other end of the
room. Frances's head was on my shoulder and her arm
inside my jacket was working magic up and down my
spine. I was sorry when we had to go back to our table,
by which time Hannaford had returned and was chatting
with Peggy.

I drank some more, happy in the knowledge that I
was used to it, but after that my memory of the entertain-
ment is something of a blur. I know I talked a great deal
and paid Frances several compliments. Hannaford's
face seemed to come and go, but it was all good fun.
Then we were leaving, the four of us, and walking up some
stairs to a landing where there were two doors. The
women each opened one with a key and Hannaford,
before he followed Peggy into a room, turned to me and
whispered, 'Let it go, John! It is paid for and quite safe!'

There was a bed and hazily I accepted that it was a
nice room and nicely furnished. Frances kissed me, softly
and with lingering sensuality, before loosening my tie.
I was dopey without feeling sleepy.

I enjoyed it, of course I did, what I can remember of
it. But it was a nothingness, meaningless.

I awoke with a slightly fuzzy head, looked down at my
naked torso and then around the room. Memories, some
clear and some hazy, began sorting themselves out into
chronological sequence. Recalling how much I'd drunk
I should have had a dreadful head, but in fact my mind
was remarkably clear. I knew what had happened.
Hannaford had engineered this from the beginning. It
had been no chance meeting with the two women, and

the only reason I could think why he should keep it to himself was that he was pretty sure I wouldn't agree. As he'd apparently spent the night with the other woman, I felt a bit disturbed. Unwittingly I had collaborated. As far as I was concerned, it didn't matter. But *he* had Sally! With a wife like her, what on earth was he doing sleeping around with a Tom, even if she were a high-class one?

I sat up. My clothes were neatly stacked on a chair near the open window. A gentle breeze ruffled the pale blue curtains. On the long dressing-table I saw a note propped against the mirror. I couldn't have missed it. I rolled out of bed and slipped on my pants before I ventured to read it.

John,
    Have had to leave. You'll find an electric razor in the bathroom. Tea is in the pot in the kitchen. Switch on the electric kettle.
    When you're ready, Tom wants you to ring him on 66536.
    Hope you had a good time.
                    Frances

I stood for a while and gave this some thought. Then I went into the bathroom and removed the stubble from my face. After a shower, I got dressed and had a cold drink from the refrigerator in the kitchen instead of bothering to make tea. Somehow I wanted to get shot of the place.

Hannaford answered the phone fairly quickly, merely giving the number.

'That you, Tom?'

'Hallo, John. Everything go all right?'

I hesitated but had to admit that I *had* enjoyed myself.

'Yes,' I said. 'Frances has gone and there's a note asking me to ring you.'

'Are you ready?'

'I'm ready.'

'Good. Give me five minutes and then go down to the street. I'll be waiting with the car.'

'Where the hell am I?'

'Not far from the club. In five minutes!'

I glanced at my watch – the first time I'd thought of doing so – and saw that it was nine-fifteen. At nine-twenty I had a final look round, checked that I hadn't lost or left anything and, from impulse, folded the note Frances had left and put it in one of my trouser pockets. Then I opened the main door of the flat, stepped into a square landing with a lift on one side, a corridor on the other and a stairway in front of me. I took the stairs, went down four flights and thence to the street.

Hannaford, true to his word, was waiting in the car. I got in beside him and he surveyed me benignly as if he were picking up someone from a convalescent home and was trying to assess his condition after treatment.

'Don't ever do anything like that again!' I said.

'Like what?'

'Like conning me. You arranged the programme without consulting me. I don't know what was in that drink we had, but that was cleverly worked out too.'

'I said you were in for a good time, didn't I? And did you have a good time?'

'I did, but that's not the point. I don't like being treated like a green half-wit, even if I am one. When I go into something, I like to know what to expect.'

True to form, he reacted in the most appropriate way. 'That was a gamble I took. I can see your point and I promise it won't happen again.' He turned and put an arm across my shoulder. 'Look! I value your friendship too much to try and "con" you, as you put it. I apologize. But you agreed to leave things to me . . .' I couldn't remember doing that '. . . and I know, if I'd told you,

you would have frozen up on it. The end result was that you had a good time. What did you think of Frances?'
'A very talented young woman.'
'Well? What harm's done? She's better off and so are you, for the experience.'
'But . . . there's Sally! What about your sleeping with the other one?'
'You're jumping to conclusions.'
'You mean you didn't have it off with her?'
'That's right. I didn't.'
I felt better after that.
He started up and we drove in silence for a few miles. Then I said, 'I have yet to see Frances when I'm in a really sober state of mind. Last night I suppose any reasonable female would have seemed beautiful to me, but she did strike me as being remarkably attractive.'
'Only the best for you, John!'
'Why does she do it?'
'Why does a footballer play football? Why does a fisherman catch fish?'
'That's over-simplifying it, isn't it?'
'I don't think so. Maybe it's the other way round and you're making it too complicated. I know what's on your mind. She's a whore, you think. But what about the women who marry for money? They're whores but are not so honest about it. She's got class and can pick and choose. She does all right out of it, so don't worry about her.'
He always seemed to have a rational answer for everything.
About twenty miles from home we were on the outside lane of a dual carriageway, following a line of cars, when it happened.
The inside lane was nose to tail. Suddenly I became conscious of a large, dark saloon breathing down our necks. Another foot or so and it would climb right inside our boot! There is an observer's mirror fitted to Hanna-

ford's car, so I could see as much of what went on behind us as he could.

We were travelling at about sixty-five miles an hour and keeping at a safe distance from the car in front. I saw Hannaford glance in his own mirror and frown. We continued for a good mile like this and then the following driver flashed his lights. Where he thought we were going, to get out of his way, beats me.

'D'you see that?' said Hannaford.

'He flashed his lights.'

From then on I was mentally driving the car as well. Again the lights flashed and for the first time I heard Hannaford use bad language — if there is such a thing these days. Then his right foot jabbed his brake pedal. With that, the driver behind, a thick-set-looking fellow with dark, bushy hair, drew back a little. But not for long. More light-flashing. A blonde woman sat next to the driver and in the rear seat I could make out a bulky male figure. Hannaford jabbed his brakes again.

'If there's one thing calculated to make me blow my top,' he said, 'it's that.'

I glanced at him. The muscles each side of his jaw were standing out and his mouth was set in a rigid, straight line. Never had I seen him like this before. I kept quiet.

Another flash from behind. More jabbing of the foot brake and consequently the brake light from Hannaford. It was the woman passenger who apparently decided it for Hannaford. Through my mirror I saw her raise two fingers, knuckles foremost. It was no 'V for Victory' sign! After that Hannaford stabbed the brakes and kept stabbing them, steadily decreasing our speed until we came to a stop and forced the other car to stop. Cars on the nearside continued to whizz by.

'What are you doing?' I asked, but he ignored me and got out. By this time there was a considerable amount of hooting. Vehicles were piling up behind, trying to get into the nearside to pass, and drivers generally were showing their frustration. I daren't open my door but I felt that Hannaford, whatever he had in mind, needed support so I stretched across and managed to clamber out through the offside door on to the central reservation. The car behind was a large grey Ford, dusty and neglected-looking. The driver had his windows down and in between revving his engine he glared angrily as Hannaford went up to him. 'What's your bloody game, mate?'

Hannaford was quite calm now. 'There seems to be something wrong with your headlights,' he said. 'They keep going on and off.'

A rasping voice from the back said, 'Funny man, eh?' The rear door opened and a male passenger, large and spivvy-looking, got out and stretched to a hefty six feet. I stole a glance at the blonde and she seemed to be anticipating some enjoyment from the interlude. Her man, her eyes appeared to say, was about to put somebody in his place.

'What's wrong with the fucking lights?' said the man who had got out of the car.

Hannaford looked at him tolerantly and spoke as if he were explaining something to a rather dull pupil.

'The lights,' he said. 'There are three possible explanations, really. One is that there's something wrong with them. Two, there's something wrong with your driver's eyesight. Or three, your driver is just a half-witted, aggressive bastard who ought not to hold a licence.'

The man spat on the ground without taking his eyes off Hannaford. Then very deliberately he placed the flat of his hand on Hannaford's face and pushed. Hannaford swayed back a little and said, 'You shouldn't have done that.'

For answer the man started to do it again, but this time Hannaford dipped one shoulder when the hand was a few inches away. There was a sudden, blurred movement,

too fast for me to follow, and the man was writhing in
agony on the ground.

The driver said, 'Hey!' and started to get out. The
woman shrieked in anger. Hannaford bent his knee
against the door and grasped the driver's arm just above
the elbow. I saw the knuckles of his hand whiten as he
gripped harder and harder, and the man drew in his
breath at the pain.

'I should stay where you are, if I were you,' said
Hannaford. 'Put him back in when he recovers and don't
flash your lights at me again.'

I think the driver got the message. He rubbed his arm
when Hannaford released him, and no doubt we should
have gone on our way without further trouble. Unfortunately the woman, who was shouting something, decided
to get out, and she opened her door right into the path of
a Rover 3000 which was about to pass on the nearside.
There was a sickening, metallic crunch and the sound of
shattering glass, followed by screeching brakes, more
crunches and glass shattering.

The driver shouted, 'You stupid cow!'

The Rover had slewed across the road and another car
behind seemed to be trying to get in on the act. Thick
and fast more cars were piling up, burning brakes and
with nowhere to go.

Hannaford said, 'Come on!' and, now unhampered by
vehicles on the nearside, I opened the passenger door of
his car and got in. He didn't make any fuss driving away,
no thundering acceleration, just a dignified withdrawal
from the scene. I turned and looked behind. The man
Hannaford had roughed up was on his knees and holding
his stomach. Two or three drivers were gesticulating,
and the driver of the offending car was pointing in our
direction. Hannaford, with a clear road behind, turned
off at the first exit.

We made several other turns and detours before we

came to the homeward route. My thoughts, confused to
say the least, were a mixture of reproach, doubt and
admiration. With him, it seemed you never knew what
was going to happen next. I could understand his being
annoyed at the hoggish behaviour of the other driver.
The same sort of thing had infuriated me many times.
But to force a halt on the fast lane was, I thought, asking
for it. Then, his subsequent actions and the handling of
the situation! He had been in control of himself the whole
time, confident in his own ability to out-think and over-
come any physical opposition. I'd guessed he was no
weakling but the way he'd pole-axed the aggressive
passenger and subdued the driver with the minimum of
effort had been a revelation. I wouldn't want him to get
upset with me!

Then I heard him chuckle and I said, 'D'you think they
took your number?'

'Who cares? I didn't open the door of their car. Let
them sort it out.'

'I don't know . . .'

'What does that mean?'

'It couldn't have gone unnoticed that you've made a
point of evading pursuit.'

'Logical tactics, unless you feel like hanging about for
another hour? Charlie back there, to cover himself,
will blame me. With that pile-up, somebody will have
called the police and they might conceivably radio for
another car to stop us and sort it out. Anyway, we're
nearly home. Stay for lunch.'

Sally, I thought, looked particularly appealing in a
sable-coloured trouser suit, and there didn't seem much
wrong with her. She kissed us both and said to me, 'You're
staying, John,' which sounded half a question and half a
statement.

What surprised me was the fact that she displayed not

the slightest curiosity about our activities of the previous
night. I couldn't decide whether this was because she
wasn't interested or because she had been trained not to
ask questions. When I enquired if she was feeling better,
her eyes moved to Hannaford before she answered. 'Yes.
Yes, thanks.'

Then we sat round the table and for some reason I was
more conscious of her than ever before. Perhaps the
cavortings of the previous night had aroused and stimu-
lated my sensual instincts. Perhaps it was some indefinable
force – electrical, primeval, call it what you will – that
emanated from her and homed in on my wavelength
with a sort of relentless purpose. And there was something
else I felt towards her that hadn't been there before: a
desire to protect.

At times I had difficulty in hiding this and, because
of it, my conversation may have become a trifle stilted.
Therefore I was not altogether surprised when Hannaford
said, 'You've got something on your mind, Captain.
What's troubling you?'

I pulled myself together and smiled. 'Not really.
I'd expected to be back earlier and I was just thinking
that I haven't paid Mrs Simmonds. It doesn't really
matter.'

Sally looked up and her eyes, large and enigmatic, as
good as said, '*That's* not it. *I* know.'

'As soon as we've finished,' said Hannaford, 'I'll take
you back. I want to call in at the shop anyway.'

Before we left I went up to the bathroom and when I
pulled out the handkerchief from my pocket the note from
Frances must have come out with it. I didn't notice it at
the time.

Half an hour later I said goodbye to Sally, and if the
kiss on my cheek was habitual the look she gave was more
serious and longer than usual.

I got Hannaford to drop me at Tyke's Point so that I could walk beside the river for the last half mile.

'See you in about a week,' he said. 'I shall be away for a while.'

CHAPTER IV

On the third day after my night club experience I got back from the Stag at about a quarter to three, and had settled down to watch the second day of the test match when there was a half-hearted ring on the door-bell, giving me the impression that whoever was calling was slightly nervous about it.

I opened the door and Sally stood there. Seeing that she was alone and there was no one in her car, my stomach took a couple of somersaults and I momentarily held my breath.

Recovering, I said, 'What a pleasant surprise,' and stood aside for her.

'You're alone, are you?' she said. 'I called by chance. I should have telephoned.'

'I'm on my own and very pleased to see you. Where's Tom?'

We went into the sitting-room where she dropped her handbag on a chair and stood looking out of the window.

'He's away with the Utility for a few days. Gone to one or two auctions up north. He was coming back today but he's been delayed.' She nodded at the television. 'Cricket! Am I interrupting?'

I moved over and switched it off.

'Of course not,' I said, and then dried up, completely lost for words. Why, I thought, was I getting so stupidly excited? Fool! I'm like a boy lovesick for some unattainable goddess. Feeling a strong urge to touch her, I put my hands in my jacket pockets.

She turned to the window again and the suspense mounted. I stared at the straight back and classical curves. Nature, I thought, had been at the peak of its form when it had designed her. Vital statistics mean little. It's the subtlety and distribution of muscle, flesh and bone which defy description.

Alone with her for the first time, and not through any fault of mine, I felt free to gaze at her openly and, as long as I kept my thoughts to myself, I could allow them to wander along erotic and indiscreet paths.

Then, without moving, she said, 'You haven't asked why I've come.'

'Was there a special reason?'

'Yes.'

When, after what seemed a lengthy pause, she hadn't enlarged on her brief affirmative, I decided to take some sort of charge of the situation.

'It's a bit early for a drink. Can I get you coffee or something?'

At last she twisted round and faced me. 'No, it's not... too early for a drink. I'd like one.' She slid into a nearby chair, sat back and crossed her legs.

'The usual?' I asked.

'Please.'

These days it seemed that providing drinks had become something of a priority. I poured a Martini for her and one for myself and we sat facing each other.

Suddenly she put her glass down.

'I just don't understand you,' she said.

I felt my eyebrows lift in astonishment.

'There's something about you. In some ways you remind me of an innocent child and in others you're as deep as they come. You went to Town with Tom. What did you do?'

So that's it, I thought. 'Is this,' I said, 'the real reason for your visit? Tom hasn't told you and you want me to?'

'Not if you don't want to.'

'It isn't a question of that exactly.' I was giving myself time to think what I could say without letting Hannaford down. 'You see, we went to a place where we had a very nice meal and a few drinks. I know what I did after that, but not what he did. I'm afraid I got rather sloshed. I presume he stayed up there until the morning, by which time I'd recovered.'

She opened her bag. 'He knew beforehand he wouldn't be back until the next day. He told me.' Reaching over, she handed me the note Frances had left me. 'I found that on the bathroom floor after you'd gone. You were to ring him at 66536. Where was that, John?'

I stared at it stupidly, consternation paralysing my vocal cords. God, I thought, how am I going to get him out of this one?

She gave me an unexpected opening. 'There's really no need to try and protect him.'

'I'm not trying. I'm in no position to, because I don't know where he went. That could be the number of the Salvation Army for all I know. As for me, as I said, I was sloshed. I woke up and found this note and I rang him. He picked me up five minutes later.'

'"Hope you had a good time",' she quoted from Frances's note. 'Did you?' Then she smiled and it completely disarmed me.

'I suppose I must have done but it didn't mean anything.'

'I hoped you would say something like that.'

'You . . . you did?'

'I'm not concerned about Tom. He can look after himself. It's you I was thinking of. You need somebody.'

Instinctively I retreated further into my chair as I

digested this bewildering new angle.

'What do you know about him?' she asked.

'Only what he's told me, and from my own personal assessment of him over quite a long time now. What is it you're trying to tell me, Sally?'

'That you don't have to worry about him.'

Her eyes said the rest and I felt the colour creep into my face. Perplexed, excited and unbelieving, I squeezed the flesh on my forehead and then kept rubbing it for something to do. In the end I said, 'But he's my friend.'

'He can stay that way.'

I had desired her before but now the temptation was unbearable. Could it be possible that she was here, practically offering herself to me? Then the name 'Hannaford! Hannaford!' kept hammering into my head and I thought of a way out.

'I'd no idea,' I said, 'no idea.' I needed time to think it over. I glanced at my watch. 'I'm expecting somebody in about ten minutes.'

'It's no good trying to brush me off,' she said, 'because I know.'

'It's not that. Although I can't understand why you . . .'

'You underrate yourself.'

'There really *is* somebody coming.' It was a lie, of course, and I wondered if she knew it.

'I'd better go, then.'

'I suppose . . . As it is now . . . Perhaps . . .'

We were standing up and she moved close to me. 'Before I leave, kiss me properly.'

Tentatively at first, I kissed her. I tried to hold back but it was no good. She clung, bending in to me, her lips, mouth and tongue soft yet demanding. I was lost to the world.

When we came up for air, she stared up at me and then lowered her eyes. I was tempted to tell her that I wasn't really expecting anybody, but the cautious instinct of years made me glance again at my watch.

At the door she said, 'Next time I'll give you a ring first.'

After she had gone I sat, unable to grasp the significance of what had happened to me and what was happening to me. As my mind began to clear I was tortured by guilt and apprehension, but this was evenly balanced by elation.

Everything she had said to me, every nuance of look or expression were etched in my memory. I went over it all again and again. It seemed inconceivable that she would want me for a lover. Had I misunderstood her? Yet her parting remark, 'Next time I'll give you a ring,' ruled that out. I was baffled by her veiled reference to Hannaford. She didn't care about him? She was more worried about me?

Had that note I had so carelessly let drop been the cause of this move of hers? Did she believe that Hannaford was innocent of infidelity? If it came to that, did I believe him now? I didn't know. I didn't know any damned thing. Fate had drawn a net around me. It was not yet complete. There was still a way out if I wanted it. But it was such a beautiful, sweet-scented net, full of delightful promises.

I put my head in my hands and said aloud, 'Ring her. It'll be easy on the telephone. Tell her it's out of the question. Tell her anything.'

I got up, poured a stiff drink and forgot about the telephone.

But that night, lying in bed and staring through the window at the wispy clouds scudding across the moon, it was Hannaford and not Sally who dominated my thoughts. What would he say if he knew – or did he know?

A man is rich, they say, when he knows he has enough.

The trouble is to stay rich in that sense, for one's needs and desires have a habit of changing.

For anybody with a troubled mind I can recommend a long, vigorous walk, especially if it's beside a river. This is what I did the next morning and by the time I got back I felt much better. I was more composed and, perhaps because I had come to a decision, clear-headed and re-solute. I now knew that I would let matters take their course, yet be constantly prepared to challenge the general pattern if I didn't like it. I refused to feel any guilt about Hannaford. After all, none of it was of my making. Furthermore, I didn't believe now that he hadn't slept with the other woman. Of course I didn't want to believe him.

In the afternoon I drove the thirty-odd miles to Hems-ford, browsed round the shops and saw a re-run of *Doctor Zhivago* at the Metropole. I hadn't seen it before. In fact I hadn't been to the cinema for years. I'd heard it was good and I also went out of curiosity because, having read the book, I couldn't imagine how they could possibly make a film of it. It was an afternoon well spent. I came away with that slightly lifted feeling that one gets after sharing the suffering and nobility of characters you can understand and sympathize with. I slept better that night.

The following morning Hannaford rang to say that he'd be over within the hour if that was convenient. He sounded his usual cheerful self.

'Sure,' I said. 'Everything all right?'

'Fine. See you, then.'

I experienced a few qualms before he arrived but I needn't have worried. He gave his slow, lazy smile and clapped me on the shoulder. 'Well, Captain, how are you?'

'Can't complain. And you?'

'Never better.' He eyed me with benevolent but sharp

appraisal. 'Do I detect a slight caginess about you that wasn't there before?'

'Caginess? I can't think why you should.'

'Nothing's happened then, nothing, that is, that concerns me? Not that I'm prying into your personal doings, my friend.'

My God, I thought, has he found out that Sally called? His next remark came as a tremendous relief.

'I should have got word to you. The day I left, the police called. It was about that fracas on the way home. Apparently they did get my number and all three are accusing me of reckless driving and assault. I made my statement and said you were a witness. Hope you don't mind?'

Tension flowed out of me. 'Of course I don't. He was the one who was reckless, driving like that right up our backside. Suppose you'd had to stop suddenly? And as for the assault, the other bloke started it. And I didn't see you hit him, although you must have done.'

'Good. I said this to the officer who saw me and the impression I got was that he was on my side.'

I made some coffee and we sat chatting for a while. Then suddenly he said, ' I've a rather unusual reproduction job for you, if you could oblige.'

I thought of Sally and felt an intense surge of gratitude towards him.

'I'll do it if I can, and this time I don't want to be paid for it.'

'Why not?'

'Because I don't. It'll be a favour to you.'

He reflected on this. 'We'll see. Anyway, you don't know what it is yet.'

'All right. What is it?'

'If I got you a really first-class colour photograph of a painting, d'you think you could copy it to pass for the original?'

'I doubt it. It might fool some but an expert would twig it. It's a question of texture and brush marks. And then, would the colour in the photograph be really true?'

'As near as makes no difference. There are close-ups, magnified, to show brush marks. And there's no reason why you shouldn't see actual works of the artist if you want more detail.'

I must say I felt flattered that he should think that I could do it.

'You want me to make a forgery?' I said.

'No, I don't. I want you to make a copy. As long as you don't sign it, it won't be a forgery as far as you're concerned. I must tell you that it is still not out of copyright for reproduction, but that needn't worry you as it won't be offered for sale.'

'What happens to it when I've done it?'

'You give it to me.'

'And then?'

'This time, if you want to know, I'll tell you, but I think it would be better if you didn't.'

'I had enough of that with Cunningham.'

'Okay. I'll be level with you. There's an element of risk for me and on no account are you to be involved. Ever been to Winterford?'

'Passed through several times.'

'There's a big, old house there called Banners Hall which until recently was lived in by an elderly widow, Mrs Lang, and her sister. At the age of eighty-five the widow died, leaving the house to her sister who'd looked after her. The sister, incidentally, is over seventy, a spinster and a really nice woman. The trouble is that after death duties there won't be much left for her. She'll have to sell the house and find somewhere else to live.

'Now before Mrs Lang died there appeared on the scene a Dr Poinge, a portly, elderly medico who knows his way around. He ingratiated himself with the old lady until she thought the sun shone out of his fat bottom. During his frequent visits he always admired three of her pictures, so much so that she gave them to him. She didn't think they had much value. Two of them hadn't, but one of them I feel sure was a Steer and he knew it, which is why he professed interest in the others as well.'

'So he's got this picture?'

'Yes. He'll hang on to it for a bit, long enough to avoid any legal complications and then put it up for auction. It should fetch quite a tidy sum.'

Here he must have noticed my puzzled expression for he said, 'I expect you'd like to know how I got on to this?'

'Naturally. Wouldn't you in my place?'

'Sure I would. About five years ago our Dr Poinge was involved in litigation over the will of an elderly lady he'd been attending. Her relatives challenged the will in court but they didn't get anywhere. At the time he was practising in Devon. Six months ago something reminded me of him, and I decided to find out what had happened to him. Through the medical register and a contact I made, I found he'd moved twice since then and was now in Winterford. I became curious, especially when I discovered that he was a regular visitor to, and had been treating, the old lady mentioned. So I engaged a private eye, a first-class chap I'd used before, to get friendly with the old ladies and find out what our doctor was up to.'

'But why go to all this trouble?'

'That's another story. Stick with this one.'

'Sorry! Carry on.'

'It wasn't long before he got into the sister's confidence and although she said nothing detrimental about Poinge – in fact she thought him a charming man – she did let out that he'd shown an unusual interest in the three pictures and that Mrs Lang had told her he could have them. This didn't bother the sister because she wasn't attached to them at all, even though they'd been in the family a long time.' He paused and said, 'With me so far?'

'I'm with you.'

'When my man told me this I smelt a nasty fat rat, and I asked him if he could get inside without any risk and photograph the pictures. He said he could and he did. I didn't ask him how, but the net result was six first-class colour photographs. Apparently the pictures were side by side in the sitting-room with the Steer in the middle.'

'But,' I interrupted, 'if it was obviously a Steer and signed by him, how was it somebody else hadn't realized it before?'

'They rarely had visitors and it was only during the last six months or so that the pictures had been hanging there. Damp had discoloured the wallpaper in a few places and rather than bother to have it re-done they'd got these out of the loft or somewhere and put them up to hide the blemishes. Not long after this, Mrs Lang was taken ill and Poinge appeared. Now, and here's the significance, on normal inspection the Steer shows no signature.' He got up and went to the door. 'Hang on a minute. I'm going to the car.'

He was back in no time with a magnifying frame and a large, square, buff envelope from which he took out a full-plate colour photograph. Whoever his man was, he certainly knew his business. They were absolutely first class.

The painting, a landscape, was in a rather tatty gilt frame but it had a freshness and an immediacy typical of Steer. It reminded me of his 'Girls Running' which I had seen in the Tate, except that it was of a cornfield with two small boys and a woman. It had the same diffused effect, as if you were looking at it through faintly frosted glass. The features were not clearly defined nor the detail particularly sharp. Steer was a prolific artist and it was by no means improbable that one of his early oils had been hidden away in obscurity for so long. I examined it closely. It would be a challenge. I had never done anything like it. The strange, vibrant stippling effect of parts of it would be difficult and the characteristic lack of definition would make it far from easy to reproduce successfully. If I *could* do it, it would be quite an achievement.

He took out another photograph. 'This is an enlargement of the right-hand lower quarter of the picture. Have a look at it through the magnifying frame.'

I slotted it into the frame and switched on the light.

'Got it?' he asked after I'd examined it for a while.

I looked up and nodded. 'Somebody's painted something out with a matching colour. When it's highlighted you can see the difference in texture, shade and brush mark.'

'And I'd wager a fortune the colouring used isn't all that fast. It'll come off when he wants it to. My man casually mentioned to Mrs Lang's sister that it was strange that this picture wasn't signed when the other two were, and she said she thought it had been signed but obviously she must have been mistaken. It was soon after this that the old lady gave Poinge the paintings and he took them away. Ten days ago she died.'

'Wait a minute. The probate people wouldn't let it go like that. If pictures were mentioned in the will they'd want them valued.'

'They weren't mentioned in the will. What's more, Dr Poinge is one of the executors.'

'You reckon he daubed a bit of colouring over the signature during one of his visits?'

'It would have been dead easy. With Mrs Lang upstairs, he could have kept her sister out of the way on some pretext. It wouldn't have taken him a couple of minutes. It's all too pat.'

'What made *you* think it was a Steer?'

'I showed the photograph to an art expert friend of mine. He said that if it was an original it was almost certainly a Steer. Bank on it, Dr Poinge doesn't do things for nothing. Well, what d'you say?'

I took out the photograph and studied it from different angles. 'You've got the exact size?'

'Thirty-two by twenty-five, from each inside edge.'

'And the frame the canvas is stretched on, how thick and how wide is it?'

'It's all there,' he said, producing another photograph. This showed the back of the painting and gave a list of measurements.

'If there'd been a lot of trees, Constable style, I don't think I could do it, but I might make a fair job of this. I'd have to practise his Impressionist style to see if I could get it right.'

'How long will it take?'

'I wouldn't like a time limit on it. I'm not all that good. Incidentally, when you've got it, what are you going to do with it?'

'I'd rather not tell you. In fact I'm not going to.'

I gave a shrug. 'There is one thing. As it's on canvas, it'll have to be stretched to the same size as the original and that will mean making a frame and pegs to the exact measurements. It will have to be weathered and treated too, to take off the newness. I just hope you know what you're doing.'

He slipped the photographs into the envelope again and put them on the table. 'It's over to you,' he said. 'I'll be away for at least a week so I'll look forward to seeing how it's going when I get back.'

It took me the rest of the day to make the frame, the slots for the pegs and the pegs for the final stretching. Preparing a canvas is a difficult and specialized job, but I had been taught the principles of it by an uncle when I was a young man. I had to improvise stretchers from stout cardboard cylinders and, although simple, it worked, keeping the tension evenly distributed throughout the canvas.

When I had adjusted the pegs for the final stretching I was less than a sixteenth of an inch out, which I thought was pretty good. Then I roughed up the back a little with fine sandpaper and made it a shade darker, but not too evenly. I prepared the painting surface and left it.

In between doing all this, sometimes I thought of Sally and sometimes of Hannaford, and I drank more than I should have done.

The next day I examined the photographs minutely, particularly the enlargements of the bottom section. After a while, and with practice, I got some idea of the technique used and the type of brushes and paint which would be most effective. Then I placed a transparent, squared grid over the picture, secured it and chalked a grid with the same number of squares on to the canvas. I was now ready to start.

I'm pretty good at line and within an hour I had reproduced much of the detail in good balance. I had concentrated intently on what I was doing and this can be tiring, so I left it and went for a drink.

A heated but friendly argument was going on when I arrived at the Stag, and George Slater grinned at me as he slid over my pint of mild.

'This is a good one,' he said and, leaning his elbows on the counter, nodded towards the protagonists, indicating that it would be worth listening to.

I turned and sipped my beer.

Bill Frogget, a ruddy-faced, middle-aged farmer, was shaking his head sadly. 'Charlie, my daftest sow's got more sense than you,' he said and shook his head again.

'Charlie' was Stanford, the village postmaster. 'Well,'

he said, 'you must have some damn bright sows. I should
think they could run your farm better than you can.'

A portly man named Reed, who apparently sided with
Frogget, leaned forward and jerked his tankard at Charlie.
'Do you honestly mean to say that you'd play Wakefield
in preference to Morris?'

'Yes, I do. Morris is too casual and he's bloody lazy.'

'It doesn't mean he's lazy because he doesn't run about
like a blue-arsed fly. And he can afford to be casual
because he knows what it's all about.'

I'd heard it all before or something similar: the merits
or demerits of players in the nearest football team of any
note. With some of them it took the place of politics or
religion and they got just as heated. Although it was
beyond me, I found it amusing to listen to them, and when
I left I felt the refreshing effect of uncomplicated normality.

But in the afternoon Sally rang. At first she just said,
'John?'

'Hallo, Sally.'

'It didn't sound like you. Anyone with you?'

'No. I haven't been in long. I was just about to start
on a canvas.'

There was a brief pause when neither of us said anything. Then, 'John, would you mind if I came over?'

'You know the answer to that. If it weren't for the
circumstances, there's no one I'd rather see. Tom called
yesterday, as you probably know.'

'Yes. This evening, about seven? All right?'

What could I say? What did I want? I wanted her and
I wanted peace of mind, but I knew I couldn't have both.

'I'll be here,' I said. 'I'll rustle up something. D'you
mind tinned salmon?'

'Of course I don't. Why not leave it for me to get
ready for you? I'll bring some salad.'

'No. I'll be the provider and the head chef. I've some of your favourite wine too.'

'See you about seven! 'Bye, John.'

As I put down the phone, warnings were being shrieked at me from every angle, but they had no effect. I had tried and I had failed. I didn't really know what was right and what was wrong any more. I didn't know anything and I was beginning not to care. I was two persons in one, playing a game of poker with each other. God knew who would win in the end!

Eventually I did manage to adopt a calm and remote discipline about it all and, after experimenting on a spare board with different methods and colour effects, I worked on the canvas without a break until five-thirty. Checking it against the photograph I wasn't displeased with it.

I had a bath and changed, and remembered to remove the five o'clock shadow. By seven I had the meal prepared – salmon salad, new potatoes, a bottle of wine – ready and waiting on the solid old gate-legged table by the window overlooking the garden.

I poured myself a stiff drink and was half way through it when she arrived. She was wearing a sleeveless white dress, plain except for a few red buttons down the front. Her hair hung straight to her shoulders, curling slightly round the nape of her slender neck. In the few seconds she stood at the door I again wondered why on earth she was interested in me. Then she was inside and had kissed me lightly on the cheek.

Her mood was entirely different from that of her previous visit. She seemed relaxed and there was an air of confidence as if she had suddenly acquired some proprietary right where I was concerned. This rubbed off on to me, and by the time I had poured her a drink and topped up my own glass I found myself staring at her with undisguised admiration.

'You look absolutely stunning,' I said.

She gave a little mock curtsey. 'Thank you, sir.'

Unexpectedly, and to my relief, conversation between us was easy and the odd silence didn't matter. When we had finished the meal she insisted on helping me to wash up, and even this boring task seemed pleasurable.

So far neither of us had attempted any move towards a renewal of the more passionate relationship of our last meeting, and Hannaford had not been mentioned. Somehow I had forced all thoughts of him from my mind and it was only when she said, 'Can I see what you're working on now?' that a suspicion of a shadow was cast on the evening. For one thing it reminded me of him and for another I was undecided whether or not she ought to see it. It was confidential between him and me. But how could I refuse? And in any case the chances were that it would mean nothing to her.

'It's only a copy,' I said.

We went into the studio and she stood for a while in front of it, comparing my work with the photograph. Then she turned and said, 'You know, you really are very good.'

'Not good enough. I can only copy. A true artist creates. I'm like the factory worker who produces from a mould.'

'I don't see it that way. You must have special skills to do something like that as well as that.'

'I'll meet you half way there but I'm still only a copier.'

We returned to the sitting-room and I was settling back into my earlier mood when I noticed a subtle change in her. It was at first no more than a strange awareness on my part of her sexuality. The message came across with increasing intensity and when, in the middle of a casual sentence, our eyes met I knew that I was about to become a most willing victim. I say 'victim' because in all fairness I had initiated none of it on this or the previous occasion.

My words trailed off as she rose from her chair and

knelt beside me. Her hand smoothed my cheek and one finger traced a line round my mouth and chin. Then her lips parted slightly and she kissed me slowly and lingeringly, moving her head from side to side. The hand which had caressed my face slid down and down, and fifty Hannafords couldn't have stopped me now. She wanted me and God, did I want her! Without a word being spoken I eased her away. We stood up and I led her upstairs.

Twice we made love within the next hour, saying very little in between. I knew it would be some time before I should be of any use to her again, but she seemed quite content to lie there in my arms. At my time of life I was surprised I had managed that, and reflecting on the little squeals of delight she had given, I felt an almost humble sense of privilege that I had been able to rouse her so.

Sanity returned slowly. Things, I knew, could never be the same. I should have to adjust, and the first thing was to rationalize this sense of guilt towards Hannaford. So, he had saved my life! But he hadn't risked his own. He was a strong swimmer and had known how to do it. It had been child's play to him. I could feel grateful without selling myself to him. On the other hand, I valued his friendship and I liked him tremendously. I admired him. Remove the carnal influence and, to be honest, I preferred his company to hers. Not that I didn't enjoy being with her but now, with passion temporarily spent, I could analyse it objectively.

'Tom must never find out,' I said.

'He needn't. Don't worry.'

I turned, resting on one elbow, and looked at her. She really was magnificent.

'Why couldn't you have married some offensive slob, someone I would detest at sight? We could have made a clean break, if you were willing.'

'In that case we'd probably never have met. Can't we

be content with what we have?'

'I shall always be on a knife edge in case he finds out.'

'I've *told* you. It wouldn't matter all that much.'

'I hear what you say but I can't understand it. If you were married to me, I should want to murder any man if he so much as pinched your bottom!'

'He's not like that. He'd understand.'

'What does that mean?'

'Don't ask me to explain, please.'

'If that's the way you feel.'

An idea suddenly struck me. 'If ever he finds out that you have come here fairly regularly, we've got to be able to give him an acceptable reason. I've never done an original portrait. Suppose I try this with you? You could sit for me and I could drag it out. He knows I'm not good at anything but copying, and we could tell him I kept making bad starts, scrapping it and starting again. We could say it was to be a surprise for him.'

She placed her hands behind her head, and the firm classical lines of her breasts stirred what was left of my exhausted virility.

'I'd like that,' she said. 'All right. Will I be . . . as I am?'

'Better not! What you have on today will be fine. Just as you were when you arrived.'

I kissed her and lay back a little more composed.

Then the doorbell rang.

Startled, I sat up and glanced at my watch. It was ten past nine. Apart from Hannaford, callers were few and far between, especially at this time. I was thinking of ignoring it when I remembered that Sally's car was parked outside, and I scrambled off the bed.

'Could it be him?' I asked.

'It shouldn't be.'

I was struggling into my slacks. 'I'll wait until you're dressed in case it *is* him. For God's sake, hurry, Sally!'

She slid off the bed and, collecting her things, went to the door. 'I'll go into the bathroom. Don't wait. Go down when you're ready.'

I heard the bathroom door shut and glanced in the mirror to make sure I was looking respectable. Then I went down as the doorbell sounded again. In the hall I hesitated. There was no shadow against the glass of the door. I thought about going out by the back door and approaching the front from the side, as if I'd been in the garden. Then I scotched the idea. If it were Hannaford, he might well have had a look round there himself when there'd been no answer to his first ring.

I opened the door and with some relief saw that it was a policeman in a flat cap, a young man with dark side-burns and a solemn face. 'Mr John Bryant?'

'Yes?'

He opened a folder he had with him and referred to something in it. 'I understand, sir, that you were in a car driven by a Mr Hannaford at about ten-thirty a.m. on the twenty-third of July on the Hemsford by-pass.'

'Yes, I was.' I made a business of looking at my watch. 'It's a bit late to be calling, isn't it?'

'Sorry if it's inconvenient, sir, but I've had a number of enquiries to square up and I'm off at ten. I intended getting here earlier but I was held up. I saw the car parked.'

'You want a statement about what happened?'

'That's right. It shouldn't take long. It'll save someone calling again or your coming to the station.'

'You'd better come in, then.'

He took off his cap as he followed me into the sitting-room and I saw him glancing round the place. I cleared a space at the table.

He took out several lined forms and we sat down. Then, with what I thought unnecessary deliberation, he wrote my full name and address, my age – I couldn't see what that had to do with it – and my occupation, which he asked about.

'What d'you want that for?' I asked.

'*I* don't, sir. It's on the form. You don't have to give it.'

'Say I'm retired.'

'Retired what?'

'Retired architect.'

After that it was plain sailing. I told him exactly what happened, with a little added emphasis on the dangerous manner of the other driver. I also made a point of describing the bellicose attitude of the passenger in the other car and the fact that he'd persisted in physical aggression after being warned to stop.

He put one or two questions, made additions to the statement and then gave it to me to read. His spelling was all right but his punctuation was way out: full stops and commas sprinkled about without any apparent reason. But it was accurate, so I signed it.

'That's fine, sir,' he said. Then, as he stood up, Sally came in.

It is amazing the volumes of understanding that can be transmitted in one involuntary, fleeting expression in the eyes. He glanced quickly from Sally to me and the wheels inside his head were saying, 'Ho, ho! I've disturbed something. No wonder he wasn't pleased to see me.'

However, he cleared his throat and nodded. 'Evening, madam,' he said and I showed him to the door. I made a point of following him to the front gate and I watched him get into his panda car and drive off.

Strolling back up the path, I wondered why on earth Sally had come down and I contemplated asking her. Then I decided against it, and when I went in I found her looking through the cupboards in the kitchen.

'I heard who it was,' she said, 'and thought you'd both probably like some coffee. I could do with some.'

This sort of eased the situation. 'You sit down,' I said,
'and I'll make it. I know where the things are. D'you
mind instant coffee?'

'Of course not. Black for me.' She squeezed my arm
and sat on one of the two bentwood chairs. 'That was
marvellous, John!'

In the process of filling the kettle I paused and looked
at her. Her eyes had an odd, preoccupied expression.

'It certainly was for me,' I said.

For another half an hour we talked, or at least I did,
answering questions mainly about myself. Then, just
before she went, she said, 'Tom will be back on Saturday.
Will Friday be all right for my first sitting? About seven?'

The 'sitting' idea seemed to make it all less involved
somehow. 'Seven o'clock on Friday,' I said.

If anybody had ever told me that I was capable of an
undercover sexual relationship with any married woman,
let alone the wife of an esteemed friend who had saved
my life, I should have laughed him to scorn. Yet it had
happened and such is the capacity of human beings for
adapting to circumstances and changes in their life
style that I had already accepted the mantle unexpectedly
thrust upon me as if I had spent a lifetime leching and
seducing women.

In mitigation I constantly reminded myself that I
hadn't made the running, that when Hannaford and I
again met I could look him in the eye and feel no shame.
Of course, with hindsight I now realize that I was adopting
the age-old principle of letting the wish be father to the
thought, but without that attitude of mind I should have
gone mad.

I worked with renewed dedication on the reproduction
and by the following evening it was finished. I varnished
it and, when it was dry, rubbed it over and heated it to
bring out the weathered cracks of an older paint surface.

Looking at it the next morning I must say I felt a most satisfactory sense of pride. As I saw it, it was good, very good. Without comparing the two paintings side by side, I reckoned it would need a sharp and experienced eye to tell the difference.

The following day I framed another canvas and waited for Sally to arrive. I didn't prepare a meal as she had phoned to say that she would already have eaten, which made me half wonder whether my culinary efforts had been quite to her liking.

She was about half an hour late, and I was getting a bit fidgety when she arrived. We clung together like a couple of young lovers and then she said, 'Have you had anything to eat?'

'I had rather a big lunch. I'll get you a drink and we'll start, shall we?'

'I feel rather excited about it,' she said. 'I really do.'

'Don't count on anything very good, or you'll be disappointed. This is just an excuse, remember?'

'I remember you told me you can copy so I've brought a colour photograph of me. Will that help?' She was already diving into her handbag and when she produced the photograph I saw that facially it could well serve the purpose. The pose wouldn't be difficult to alter.

'Fine,' I said. 'This should make all the difference.' Then a thought suddenly crossed my mind. 'Does Tom ring you when he's away?'

'Not very often, and then usually because he wants something.'

'When he gets back, doesn't he ask you what's been happening, what you've been doing?'

'No. He waits for me to tell him. Sometimes I don't.'

I shook my head at this strange relationship.

'Why talk about him? He's all right,' she said.

After an hour there was very little detail, but the line

and balance were reasonable, and I felt I'd made a good start. She was very patient and when I said that that was it for the day, she came round to look at it.

'Have I got as good a figure as that?' she said

'Better. I'm afraid I can't hope to do you justice.'

'You're either biased or flattering. It is exciting though, isn't it, watching it grow?'

We made love again, and afterwards lay there without interruption until it was time for her to go.

'It'll be over a week before I can come again,' she said, and I felt the first pangs of the bitter-sweet nature of our clandestine love.

When she had gone there was a compulsion to commence work again on the portrait and, with the aid of the photograph, I produced her features and her expression. And somehow, and I know the idea is absurd, it seemed that my hand was guided in its task.

CHAPTER V

When Hannaford came the following day he was delighted with the reproduction.

'I must confess I didn't expect it to be as good as this,' he said. 'Can I take it with me?'

I looked at it for a while without answering. Then I must have had a rush of blood to the head. 'Tom,' I said, 'I've been thinking about this. You're not going to sell it as a reproduction, are you?'

'No, I'm not.'

'What are you going to do with it?'

'I'm keeping that to myself.'

'My guess is that somehow you're going to try and swap them over. Am I right?'

'On the button!'

'Let me tell you something. It'll be no good just putting it into the outer frame. The whole canvas will have to be transferred on to the original inner frame. The wood on this one will shriek at him if he's got any sense.'

'I was going to dull it down a bit, and I don't think he'll look at the back much.'

'It won't work. It'll be a tricky job and if you want to make a go of it there'll be last-minute adjustments. You can't do that. The whole operation may take a couple of hours. I'm coming with you.'

He surveyed me seriously. 'I've already told you. You're not to become involved any more. I'm going to get into his house when he's not there, and I can't have you doing that.'

'This is a specialist job, and I can't even advise you without seeing the original. It's all got to be done properly or you're wasting your time. I take it you do want him to be deceived?'

'Of course, otherwise I'd pinch the damn thing as it is. The first time I want him to know about it is when he thinks of selling it, probably in about a year's time.'

'Won't he find out something's wrong when he goes to wipe away whatever he's covered the signature with?'

'I expect he will, but he's not likely to shout about it. There'd be too many awkward questions asked.'

'Suppose he's already uncovered the signature?'

'In that case I'll forge it on yours. I think you'll agree that I could do that.'

'With a brush?'

'Oh yes. I've had a look at other works of his and had some practice.'

I might have guessed he wouldn't overlook something like that.

'It makes no difference. I've got to compare mine with the original to see if any alterations are needed. I'm

surprised at you for not realizing this. I'm coming with
you.'

'Oh no, you're not.'

'You don't have it, then.'

'You can't mean that?'

'I do mean it. Get me in there, find it and I'll do it
for you.'

'But if anything happened?'

'That's your speciality. Work out a way of getting me
to it with the minimum of risk and provide me with a
let-out.'

It was some time before he answered. 'All right. Keep
it until I'm ready. I'll be in touch.'

Long, long afterwards I was to ask myself why, if he
hadn't wanted me to accompany him, had he bothered
to tell me about Poinge at all, why he hadn't merely
requested a reproduction from the photograph and left
it at that!

I was beginning to realize what is meant by a 'split
personality'. I would think of Sally, and mental pictures
and memories of us together excited and invigorated me,
turning aside the need for excuses. Then it was Hannaford
and the deception I was playing on him.

All my life I had shunned any form of dishonesty, but
then I had never before yearned so much for something
which was there for the taking. And, I argued, it was true
that I should not have yielded if I hadn't allowed Sally
to convince me that Hannaford wouldn't mind, and if I
hadn't so willingly accepted the conclusion that he himself
had slept around more than a little.

I worked on Sally's portrait, either from the photograph or from memory, and I paid the occasional visit
to the Stag. On one of these, George Slater signalled with
his thumb, indicating that he wanted a confidential word
at the end of the bar. I wandered along and he put his

head close to mine.

'Chap came in yesterday asking if I knew of a John Bryant hereabouts. I made out I was puzzling over it and decided to say that I didn't. I said, "Does he live round here?" and he said, "I'm not sure." I said, "Is he a friend?" and he said he was. Then I asked him who I should say was enquiring after this Mr Bryant if he turned up, and he said, "Oh, just a friend." This made me pleased I hadn't put him right. I can't say I took to him much.'

'What was he like?'

'Biggish chap, smart, middle-aged. I would have taken another look at him only we suddenly got busy, and then he'd gone.'

'I can't think of anybody who'd be asking after me, anybody, that is, who doesn't already know where I am.'

'I did right then?'

'You did, and many thanks. What are you going to have?'

Hannaford rang the next morning to ask if it was all right for him to call about two. I said it was.

As soon as he came in, he said, 'Tomorrow! I'll pick you up at seven. He'll be out playing bridge.'

'Won't there be anybody else there?'

'No. He lives on his own behind and above his surgery. He has a daily and the usual staff, but they won't be there then. I'll bring you some different clothes to wear and we'll go in my car.'

'Why the different clothes?'

'In case anybody near by sees you.'

'Is it going to be as tight as that?'

'It shouldn't be tight at all. I don't anticipate any trouble. However, Captain, we must prepare for the unexpected, and it is better that no one should be able to identify you as having ever been near the place. That's all there is to it.'

'You've got it all planned out?'

'Pretty well. Be here ready at seven tomorrow and leave the rest to me. I presume you'll bring the equipment you need.'

'Sure. Pliers, a small hammer, a knife, brushes and paint and anything else I think of.'

'Right. I'd better push off now. Things to do.'

'Before you go, hear this. At the Stag yesterday the landlord said some fellow had been enquiring about me.'

'A friend of yours?'

'He said he was but I'm damn sure he wasn't. He wouldn't give his name to the landlord, who acted with commendable discretion. Said he couldn't place me. He didn't like the look of the chap.'

'Did he describe him?'

'Nothing to catch on to. Biggish, smartly-dressed and middle-aged. I was wondering . . . Could it have been Cunningham, the phoney property salesman?'

'Why should he want to see you? I've already written to him in your name telling him you'll get in touch if you're interested and he replied agreeably enough, hoping he would hear again before long.'

But something was still niggling me. I didn't know what it had all been about, why I had been recruited to get the man to the house in Marchester and then give him the drugged drink.

'Suppose it is him,' I said, 'and he finds out where I live?'

'So what? You've moved. You don't owe him any explanation. If he is trying to contact you and by some fluke does find you, stall him. Tell him you've got to go out and ask him to come back tomorrow. Then get in touch with me.'

'There's one other thing. A policeman called about the accident. I made a statement which coincided with yours and was true, and he seemed satisfied. You heard any more?'

'No, and I doubt I shall. Now, we've more important matters to attend to. Tomorrow at seven, okay?'

'Okay,' I said and hoped it sounded convincing.

I awoke to the sound of pouring rain thudding on to a flat roof and trickling along the guttering. Through the open window I could smell the damp earth and the added fragrance of the garden. I got out of bed, pulled the window to and glanced at my watch. It was seven-thirty.

An hour later I had washed and shaved, and was having a light breakfast of cereal when Sally rang.

'You on your own, John?'

'This time in the morning! Of course. I've been thinking of you.'

'I hoped you were. I wondered if Tom was with you. He left about an hour ago and said he was seeing you some time today.'

'He's coming this evening.'

There was a distinct pause. 'This evening?'

'That's right. You sound concerned about something.'

'Well, no, except that he's been behaving very oddly. I can't explain so don't ask me to try. Is he coming for any special reason?'

I hated lying to her but I had to. 'Not that I know of.'

'You sound as if you do know something.'

I gave a light laugh. 'Not half as much as I'd like to. Don't go imagining things. There is one thing I want to know.'

'What's that?'

'If you've missed me?'

'Yes, I have. In about three or four days he'll be away for a while.'

I had this mixed-up feeling again. 'We'd better watch

it. I've heard some rather incriminating conversations over crossed lines. You sure you're okay?'

'Sure. See you!' She put the phone down.

Hannaford arrived with a bundle of clothes over one arm and carrying a large case. He strode into the sitting-room, dropped the case and flung the clothes on to a chair. 'Try these for size.'

I picked up a pepper-coloured jacket and trousers and, after surveying them critically, slid out of my own jacket and tried on the one he'd brought. This was a reasonable fit but I didn't much care for it.

'That,' he said, 'is very good. Not at all like you. With a few other embellishments, nobody will recognize you in it. Wear your oldest brown shoes.'

I put on the trousers and they fitted well enough. Then he gave me a hideous, spotted bow tie.

'You want me to wear *that*?' I asked

'Sure. Try it and don't judge the final result until we've finished.'

I shrugged resignedly, put it on and winced at my reflection in the mirror.

'Now turn and face the light.'

He took from the case three small false moustaches. I could see they were the pukka thing and not the cheap variety people lark about with. After some consideration he chose one and pressed it firmly and smoothly on to my upper lip.

He then handed me a pair of horn-rimmed spectacle frames with no glass in them. They were a trifle too large and inclined to slip down, but he had the answer to that. Producing a small tube, he punctured it with a pin and squeezed a small knob of plastic solder between the hinge joints. He opened them just wide enough to spring against the side of my head and put them on to the table.

'This is the most difficult part,' he said. 'Can you sit

on an upright chair?'

I pulled one out and when I sat down I saw that he was holding a bottle of dark lotion.

'This will easily come off when you wash your hair,' he said, 'so don't worry about it spoiling your looks permanently!'

My hair is thick and springy and with quite a few grey streaks. The parting is on the left side. He rubbed this stuff well into it and, whipping a comb from his top pocket, parted it on the right side. Then he smoothed it back at an unusually sharp angle. After he'd wiped round my forehead with a cloth he'd also brought with him, he stood back and said, 'Take a look at yourself now.'

I should never have believed I could have been so transformed. The person staring back at me wasn't me surely? With the change of hairstyle, the moustache, spectacles and the clothing, even the bow tie seemed to fit in somehow. I was noticeable but unrecognizable, which was what Hannaford wanted.

'Where did you learn a trick like this?' I said.

He gave a throaty laugh. 'Does it matter? It's just a question of imagination, application and experience.'

'Are you going to disguise yourself?'

'Not quite as much as you. However, you're not quite finished yet. We want your arm in a sling. You're going to be a patient visiting the doctor after surgery hours and apparently by appointment. Any risk for you is to be cut to the absolute minimum.'

'But you said he'd be out playing bridge?'

'He will be, but his next-door neighbour won't be aware of that or the people across the road, and they might see you. His house is on a corner and I happen to know that he has nothing to do with anybody living round him.'

'Has he a burglar alarm?'

'Yes, but that won't be any bother. I'll have it switched off by the time I let you in. Do exactly as I tell you and, barring a thousand-to-one chance, there'll be no trouble, no trouble at all.'

He fixed a broad arm sling on my right arm, and this also served the purpose of concealing the top half of the rolled-up canvas and the cardboard stretchers I had made. The bottom half I tucked into the front of my trousers and the buttoned jacket did the rest.

I didn't recognize the dark blue Marina outside and, anticipating my question, he said, 'Belongs to a car dealer friend of mine. It'll go back to his parking lot tonight.'

I noticed that he'd drawn on a very thin pair of skin gloves, and as we drove along I thought about this and other things. Could it be? Surely not! But could it be? Was he a crook, a real crook? If so, what had I let myself get mixed up in? Yet there was his business? No, I made myself think, I'm getting it all out of proportion. Maybe what he intended now was illegal but was it morally wrong? I refused to consider it further.

It took us an hour to reach the quiet suburban area in Winterford where Dr Poinge ran his practice.

'The house is on the next corner on the right,' said Hannaford. 'I'll drive slowly by. Take a look.'

I couldn't see much of it because it was surrounded by a six-foot red brick wall. There was a wrought-iron gate with a brass plate. Crazy paving led to the front door. I did notice that the house next to it was some thirty feet away and screened by a high hedge and a gnarled and rampant tree.

We turned a corner and another, and then Hannaford stopped.

'Walk up there,' he said, 'first left, left again and it will bring you back to the house. It should take you about twenty minutes. When you get there, kid yourself you're expecting treatment.'

'Suppose somebody is in, and it's not you?'

He shook his head. 'Oh, ye of little faith! What's

easier than asking if a Freddie Fitch or a Harry Hobley
lives there? But don't worry, it'll be me. If you don't get
an answer straightaway, wait.'

I got out of the car and watched him drive off.

Apart from a chubby little man with a big dog, I didn't
see anybody after that. The dog strained at his leash with
what I took to be friendly interest and the man said,
'Good evening.'

I said, 'Good evening to you,' and walked on.

The houses I passed were pleasant, with well-kept
gardens, but it all seemed dead, as if the residents shunned
each other's company and were frightened to get involved.
They may, of course, have been peering out from hidden
positions in their domestic strongholds but I didn't see
them.

I glanced at my watch as I approached my objective
and found that once again Hannaford's calculations were
more or less dead on. Twenty-one-and-a-half minutes I'd
been.

A few more paces, open the gate and up the path!

I was about to ring the bell when the door opened and
Hannaford ushered me in.

'Good man!' he said and, as I gazed about me in the
wide, green-carpeted hall, he nudged my arm. 'Come on!
You haven't time to look around. I've found it. Incidentally, don't touch anything.'

'You've found it already?'

I glanced through the open doorway of a waiting-room
as we passed.

'I guessed it wouldn't be hanging on one of the walls
and it's not something you can shove in a drawer. I
whipped quickly through the main rooms and bedrooms
until I found this.'

He was leading me down some steps, and we entered a
small cellar-cum-store, windowless and cluttered with the
usual assortment of things that are put in such places. I

could just about see this by the light through the doorway
from above, but when he shut the door there was total
blackness. He switched on a light which came from a naked
bulb at the end of a brown, twisted flex suspended from the
ceiling. The framed picture was leaning against a large,
fabric-covered chest.

'It was over in the corner with the other two, covered
up. I put it where it is now. We mustn't hang about. Can
you work in gloves?'

'I'd rather not. I must feel what I'm doing.'

I slipped my canvas and the stretchers from the sling,
which I took off. Then I examined the original thoroughly
before I made a move, and I was relieved to see that Poinge
hadn't yet uncovered the signature. But I agreed with
Hannaford. I would have gambled heavily on it being a
genuine Steer.

Removing the outer frame was easy, but before I
started on the canvas on the main frame I unrolled my
copy and compared it for size.

'We're going to lose about a sixteenth of an inch all
round,' I said, 'but I don't think it'll be noticed.'

'How long will it take?'

'I'll have some idea in a minute.'

I began working with pointed pliers and a thin screw-
driver on the surrounding tacks. Each tack, as I got it out,
I handed to Hannaford to hold and I wasn't going to
hurry despite his obvious impatience. When the final
tack was removed, I still had to be ultra careful not to tear
the ageing canvas, which here and there clung to the wood.
Eventually it was off and I spread it flat on to the floor.

Half an hour later, using my stretchers, the small hammer and the original tacks, I had transferred my picture
to the frame and had trimmed the slight waste. Finally
I tapped in the triangular pegs in the corners. Then I
compared the two, side by side.

'What d'you think?' I asked.

'Bloody marvellous! You're a genius, my old friend.'

'The blue in places isn't absolutely right but, without the original, I doubt very much whether he'll notice.'

'I'm damn sure he won't.'

I took a small bag from my pocket and sprinkled dust from it on to the back of the canvas, rubbing it in and making it patchy until it closely resembled the original.

'I like it,' he said. 'I like it.'

'He might notice any change in his own work, though,' I said and with a tube of poster paint and a small brush I darkened slightly the small area which corresponded to that covering the signature on the original.

Hannaford looked at me admiringly. 'A really professional touch that! Will it take long to dry?'

'Not long. I'll put it in the main frame and you can replace it how and where you found it. Don't let anything touch the bit I've just done, that's all.'

Another ten minutes and we were ready to leave, and I must confess I'd got a kick out of it.

'How did you fix the burglar alarm?' I asked before he opened the door for me.

'Unscrewed the positive terminal just above your head.'

I looked up and saw a couple of wires disappearing somewhere above the door.

'How did you get in without starting it off?'

'The simple approach. The windows are alarmed as well. A large sheet of thick, brown paper, some sticking compound and a good glass cutter, and all I had to do was step inside. Sometimes doors from the hall are alarmed as well, but I happened to know that these aren't. It isn't a good system. But we're wasting time. You walk back the way you came and keep on until I pick you up. Right?'

I adjusted my sling and walked down the path to the road. Unless they were peering from behind curtains, again there was no one to see me and I strolled calmly down the road, a private patient nursing an injured arm. It had been a good plan, well thought out except for the forcible entry. That wouldn't go unnoticed.

Hannaford, who drew alongside twenty minutes later, provided the answer. We had driven several miles when he turned down a lane and stopped by an algae-covered pond. I watched him get out, look about him for a few minutes and then casually take a few white boxes and some small bottles from his jacket pocket. These he threw well into the pond and returned to the car.

'Drugs, my old friend,' he said. 'Pinched to cover the real purpose of our visit. The police will be looking for an addict whose supply has run out or a pusher with a ready market.'

In Tossington he dropped me again and I walked on for about fifteen minutes before he picked me up in his own car.

For a few miles he made all the running conversationally until he said, 'John, my friend, there's something on your mind.'

'Yes. You've been on my mind. I expect I'm a bit dumb in many ways but I'm not so stupid that I can't put two and two together where you're concerned. I accept that the property chap and this doctor had it coming, but you're far too accomplished for these to have been one-off jobs. You must know quite a bit about burglar alarms for one thing, and then the way you planned it all! Are you a professional?'

I turned my head and saw him give a lop-sided grin.

'Yes, I'm a professional. I'll tell you about it when I get to your place,' he said.

CHAPTER VI

The church clock was showing eleven-fifteen as we passed through Little Tarling. Another twenty minutes and we were pulling on to my drive. At that hour I am usually thinking of bed, but not now.

'Sally expecting you home any special time?' I asked as we went in.

'No. When I arrive. I told her not to wait up.'

I settled him with a drink and, while I was getting rid of my disguise and rinsing the colouring out of my hair, this new aspect of him which I had suspected and which he had now confirmed began fermenting unpleasantly in my mind.

A housebreaker? A thief? If I had been less trusting I should have rumbled it before. On that very first day after he'd rescued me, he'd given me a clue. 'What's your line of business?' I had asked, and he had answered, 'It could be crime for all you know.'

This second job, he hadn't suggested it. I had volunteered to go with him, but if it hadn't been for my involvement with Sally I wouldn't have considered it for one moment.

Suppose she was in it with him? Suppose the build-up of the darker sides of Cunningham's and the doctor's characters was untrue?

When I rejoined him in the sitting-room I was in a really nasty mood and I hadn't felt like that for a long, long time.

'So,' I said, 'you admit now to being a housebreaker and a common thief by profession. Is that it?'

For a few moments he toyed with his drink, swirling it round in his glass and staring down at it. Then he looked

up at me with the kindly but sorrowful expression of a
schoolmaster whose favourite pupil hasn't quite got his
sums right.

'You're annoyed, John – understandably, I suppose.
Get yourself a drink and allow me to explain.'

I could feel him watching me as I filled my glass and,
when I sat down, he said, 'Are the windows shut?'

'Yes.'

'And the back door locked?'

'It is.'

'Tell me something. Why did you volunteer to come with
me tonight?'

I hadn't an answer to that, at least not one I could
give him, and whether he'd intended it or not he'd swiftly
put me on the defensive.

'Well,' I said. 'Well, I told you. I considered that to
pull it off you needed me there.'

'To pull it off? Exactly! You knew what I intended was
illegal, whatever Poinge had done. For some reason you
trusted me then, for which I am honoured, and you were
satisfied that he deserved it.'

'Yes, but . . .'

'Sorry, John. I should be answering the questions, not
you. I was a bit surprised when you suggested I was a
common thief. Anybody else but you and I should have
told him to go to hell.'

I was no longer indignant. In fact he had so turned
the tables that I actually felt ashamed of myself.

'Perhaps I was a bit hasty,' I said, 'but you did agree
that you are a professional.'

'A professional, yes, but not a thief in the true sense.
At least I don't think I am.'

'The law would say you are.'

'The law would say Poinge isn't, but he is. There is
often a wide gulf between legality and justice. As a nation,
we've done our share of thieving in the past, except that

it was called colonization. We even destroyed the homes
and livelihood of the inhabitants of a small Pacific island
to get the mineral wealth there. When the poor devils
took it to court, they hadn't a case according to the law.'

'We gave them something, didn't we?'

'A pittance, conscience money. And that doesn't alter
the fact that the island wasn't ours in the first place.
Anyway, we weren't talking about islands. I was going to
tell you about myself.'

I nodded at his glass. 'D'you want a refill first?'

'No, thanks. Where shall I begin? Yes, perhaps from
the time I qualified as a solicitor.'

'*You* are a solicitor?'

'Yes. Nothing so remarkable about that. I don't
practise now. For three years I was with a certain firm
and it didn't take me long to realize that under their
respectable cover some of the partners were as twisted as
corkscrews. Their sole object was to make money by
whatever means, as long as it was within the framework
of the law. I was particularly good at defending criminals
in the lower court, most of whom were as guilty as hell.
Consequently this became my speciality, but I noticed
other things. Simple, honest clients were being subjected
to delaying tactics to increase their bills. Letters were
sent unnecessarily, difficulties were created when they
need not have existed. My side of it seemed clean by
comparison but I began to be sickened by the whole
set-up.

'I was a good mixer.' Here he gave way to some inner
thought. 'How drink can loosen some people's tongues,
people who imagine you are one of them! I could name
at least six councillors who should be behind bars for
receiving stolen property from a Corporation Department.
I could name others who think nothing of signing in to
claim their attendance money at a council meeting and
then leaving.

'Disregarding the rapists and the violent types, I can think of dozens of genuine criminals who are no more dishonest than many of your Crombie-coated VIPs. But don't get me wrong. Not all professional men or administrators are bent – far from it. I'm only concerned with those who are, the officials who will see a hard-working man go out of business if their palms are not greased to allow a building project to go through, and the con-men who "legally" swindle gullible people out of their life's savings. Those, and only those, are my victims. The law can't touch them but I can.'

'You mean,' I said, 'that you select the, shall we say, bad eggs to deal with?'

'I mean just that. I take from people who deserve it, not honest people who have worked hard for what they have. I keep what I get, except for the odd occasion when I can trace some of my clients' victims, as in the case of Cunningham.'

'What did you get out of him?'

'Before I tell you that, I should go back to what I was saying earlier. I left the firm of solicitors I was with. I could have gone to another firm but that didn't appeal to me. I didn't know what I wanted to do. It had to be different. Perhaps I had something of my father in me. I haven't told you about my parents. They were both killed in the war, my mother in a raid over London and my father as a Battle of Britain pilot, the battle that he and those like him won so that years later people who ought to be crawling from under stones could swindle and thieve their parasitic way through life without the risk of being caught.

'I knew what I didn't want: anything ordinary, unadventurous and without the slightest element of risk. I'm no business man in the true sense. Industry didn't appeal to me. I was too keen on my creature comforts to tramp over Africa or somewhere, seeking out the

unknown. I suppose I was really looking for an enemy
to pit my wits and ability against.

'For two months I travelled abroad and on one of my
journeys I met a character who introduced me to smuggling. He was clever and the idea appealed to me. We
formed a partnership, a successful one, and brought in
quite a bit of the stuff.'

'Stuff?'

'Diamonds. Easy to conceal and a very small quantity
is worth a lot. For six months we prospered. He got hold
of them and we took it in turns to breach the Customs.
He wanted me to carry them through every time but I
wasn't having that. Then one day we had a narrow escape
– or at least he did. The diamonds were packed in cotton
wool and concealed in a spring-loaded compartment in
the heel of one of his shoes. It was our usual way of getting
them in. He went through all right but I was searched,
and the first place they went to was the heel of my shoe.
Fortunately I wasn't wearing my adapted pair so they
drew a blank. But it warned us that someone had tumbled
to us or had been given the tip-off. We had always kept
apart on our trips, but that was enough and we called it
a day.

'By that time for various reasons I wasn't sorry. I'd
become a bit disenchanted with him. He wanted me to
stay. He'd got an idea for real estate which was foolproof, he said. But I knew what I was going to do and I
was going to do it on my own.'

'Are you sure you won't have another drink?' I asked.

'No, thanks. I've got to drive home soon. As I was
saying, I knew what I was going to do. Basically the idea
was very simple. I would establish a business and run it in
strict conformity with the law, a dignified business above
reproach which would stand any investigation by tax
officials or the police. For my purpose I needed a business
where the goods sold did not come from warehouses or

manufacturers, as that would involve set profits and all that goes with them. Although I was going to own the business, I would have an honest manager to run it and pay him a good salary. A high-class antique shop was the answer, for reasons you will see in a minute.

'The second part of my plan would not bear official investigation. With the experience I had gained of the darker side of respectability, I decided to go in for crime. I had a retentive memory, the patience and ability to prepare the ground and the nerve to carry it out.'

I nodded in silent agreement with that.

'I also had enough "clients" to make a start, selected people who would not make a fuss at the disappearance of their ill-gotten gains. It all worked like a dream. It is surprising how careless some "respectable" rogues are. Nearly always I used the method of substitution. If it was cash, I would take only the bottom half of a pile, leaving accurately-cut paper in its place. That way the chances were that the displacement would not be noticed until long after the event took place. If it was diamonds, which is a common means of hoarding inflation-proof wealth, I would substitute good paste and leave the genuine ones on top.

'From the beginning I kept a file of newspaper cuttings, comprehensive, indexed and cross-referenced. I have it locked away now. There was mention of a man named Marshall and one of his heartless schemes about a year ago. There was also reference to it in *Nationwide* on television. The man you knew as Cunningham, this Marshall, and my early smuggling partner are one and the same. I suppose it is a coincidence that he should come to my attention, but if there weren't coincidences the word wouldn't be in the English language.

'There is a private enquiry agent I use – I mentioned him when we were talking about our mercenary doctor. He's good and he's tight-lipped, but even he has no idea

why I need the information he gets for me. Sometimes I
make my own enquiries through contacts I have made.
In Cunningham's case I knew he used to accumulate
diamonds and keep them on his person. I merely had to
establish that he still did this. It didn't take me long to
find them.'

'In the heel of his shoe?'

'Exactly! They would either be there or in a special
pocket, indiscernible in the shoulder padding of his
jacket. He had a thing about the stuff being stolen and
reckoned that the safest place was on him somewhere so
long as it was concealed well enough. No doubt he had a
look immediately after leaving hospital and was satisfied
that all was in order. If he'd known I'd had anything to
do with it, he would have looked again. The night we
both went to the club I disposed of the proceeds quite
legitimately for fifteen thousand pounds.'

'Fifteen thousand!' I said in astonishment. 'Couldn't
they be identified?'

'No. That's the beauty of it. The Israelis have invented
a system for classification based on light refraction but as
yet it's too costly to operate. Incidentally, six thousand
went towards compensating those of his victims I could
trace.'

'How does all this help you with your antique business?'

'It enables me to buy good stuff without haggling. I
usually manage to get bills of sale knocked down to show a
legitimate profit. The business cannot fail to prosper and
apart from that I have enough stacked away somewhere
else.' He sat back and eyed me shrewdly. 'That's my
story, John. You're the only one, apart from myself, who
knows it.'

In a way I wished he hadn't told me but in another I
was glad he had.

'Why have you trusted me like this?'

'For three reasons and I'll give them in order of

priority. First, we've been friends long enough now. I know you and I know I can. Secondly, I would deny it and no one would believe you. Lastly, on the only occasions you could supply the semblance of proof, you yourself were involved. I may add that it's the last time you will be.'

'The first reason is good enough,' I said.

'I know that,' he said. 'I hope this won't make any difference to our friendship.'

'Not on my part. I expect a lot of people would like to do the same if they had the guts. Has Sally any idea?'

'Not a hint. What's more natural than for me to go round the country buying?'

'What happens now?'

'If it's all right with you, we'll carry on as if you didn't know.'

He left shortly after, taking the Steer with him, and as he drove off he said, 'See you soon . . . and thanks!'

CHAPTER VII

A man had saved my life. Then, by the strength of his personality and his friendship, he had dragged me clear of the slough of despond from which I had been struggling to escape. Against all conceivable possibility, I was now not only having an affair with his wife, I was almost besotted with her. For God's sake, what sort of a man was I?

That was enough to cause problems without the discovery that he was a criminal – with some moral justification no doubt, but still a criminal.

I knew instinctively that the things he had told me were true. I knew also that the best course for me to adopt would be to cut myself free from both of them. Finally I knew that whatever the consequences, I would do nothing. I would go along with things as they were.

So when Sally arrived the next day I had once again adjusted to a changing situation. She was very impressed with the portrait.

'Do I look as – what's the word? Isn't it a bit flattering?'

'Far from it. It doesn't do you justice yet and I doubt if it ever will.'

I looked at it again critically and realized how much I had unconsciously put into it. It was already a portrait of a good-looking woman, but there was more, even now. The words 'enigmatic' and 'seductive' came to mind and inexplicably there was a latent sense of tragedy. That wasn't all. Something else emanated from it but I couldn't place it.

She sat for me for an hour. We had a drink and then made love. I consoled myself with the thought that it was the portrait now. She was here for that and it was materializing for anyone to see. What happened in between was personal, no business of anybody else nor harm to them. I revelled in my re-awakened sexuality and shut everything else from my mind.

Sally came the next day and the next. As we lay on the bed, her head on my shoulder, she said, 'Tom will be home tomorrow and he won't be going away again for several weeks.'

'We must be grateful for what we can get. He mustn't know.'

She was silent, and then, 'How long can you make the portrait drag out?'

'A long time yet. I can have made several false starts. You'll ring me though, won't you?'

'I'll ring you,' she said.

The next morning I went to the Stag. As I pushed through the door of the one and only bar I was greeted with a burst of laughter which subsided suddenly to a clearing of throats and one or two embarrassed glances in my direction. I didn't need a brick wall to fall on me to realize that I, or something to do with me, was the cause of their mirth. However, I ignored it, acknowledged the friendly greetings and ordered a pint of bitter.

The bar had thinned out considerably when George in a confidential whisper said, 'See anything of that fellow I mentioned?'

'No. Has he been in again?'

'Not since, no.'

We were some distance from those remaining in the bar and I gave him a steady, calculating look. 'What were all the guffaws about as I came in?'

He looked down at the counter and wiped it with a cloth.

'A bit of a joke someone cracked.'

'Something to do with me?'

'Sort of, but nothing harmful. Anybody else and they'd have pulled his leg openly.'

'Why couldn't they pull my leg, then?'

'Probably didn't know how you'd take it.'

'How did I come into it?'

An amused grin spread over his face. 'Guess they were envying you a bit. One or two of them have seen the young woman who's visited you on and off lately. She's something, according to them. It all started from that and you can guess the rest.'

I nodded. 'Actually I'm painting her portrait.'

'None of my business. I'd like to see it though, when it's done.'

When I got home the incident in the pub rather niggled and I realized how stupid it had been of me to think that no one in the village would notice that Sally was calling on me so often. She was hardly the type of woman any healthy male would let pass without a second glance. After several visits conjecture would be the natural outcome.

I wasn't unduly worried because the portrait was there as proof. I went into the studio, placed the canvas on the easel and kept comparing my work with the photograph Sally had supplied. But photographs can only give an impression. The portrait, even in its unfinished state, had a significance unrevealed in the photograph.

Then I heard the distant sound of the front door bell. It wasn't Hannaford's ring. It wasn't Sally – she would have telephoned first.

I took my time strolling through the house and the bell gave a single peal as I reached the door. I opened it and immediately had to camouflage my dismay. There in front of me was the property fellow, Cunningham. Before, he had been all geniality. Now, except for a disconcertingly purposeful look in his eyes, his face was blank.

'Mr . . . er . . . Cunningham?' I said.

'And Mr Bryant.'

I glanced quickly at my watch. 'I'd ask you in,' I said 'but it's not really convenient now. In any case, I told you I'd be in touch with you as soon as I was ready.'

'So you did. But you'd better make it convenient. I've come a long way.' A nasty edge on his voice seemed to become nastier, and we stared at each other for a few seconds.

'Well?' I said.

'You're not so hospitable as you were at the previous residence where I found you.'

Then he brushed past me and I thought it expedient to shut the door. Showing none of the courtesies of a normal visitor, he strode through the hall, leaving me to follow, and as the door to the sitting-room was open, this is where he led me. His arrogant, confident manner was slightly intimidating and, while I wasn't exactly afraid, I did feel a little apprehensive. Sizing him up, I didn't reckon he was the physical type and he was a bit smaller than me. But you never knew what people were like under their clothes. Perhaps he was trained in something or other and was used to the rough stuff when necessary. I'd never been aggressive by nature, and even during boyhood had managed to steer clear of giving or receiving a real blow in anger.

With an assumed firmness I said, 'You've got a nerve!'

'That makes two of us,' he said, his eyes darting about, taking in everything. 'You're the first bastard who's ever fooled me. I could've sworn you were the easy, inoffensive type.'

'I don't know what you're talking about. You'd better leave.'

'I'm not leaving, chum, until I get 'em back.' He squinted slightly as he looked at me. 'I must say it was bloody clever. I'll give you that. You'd probably have got away with it too if I'd left it a few months longer to sell.'

'Sell? Sell what? Are you talking about this Spanish business?'

He took a deep breath and folded his arms.

'I'll give you a few minutes to produce them. Let's have 'em and I won't ask you how you knew I'd got them or how you knew where they were. Five minutes! After that I'll tear the place apart and you, if necessary.' He checked his watch.

'You've obviously got some imaginary grievance,' I said. 'What am I supposed to produce?'

'All right, I'll tell you how I know. You get me to come to some place you've leased for a few weeks on the pretext of property negotiation. We come to an arrangement. You give me a drink just before I leave. Then I find I've got a flat tyre which allows time for the knock-out drops to work. It also means you've got an accomplice because you couldn't have let the tyre down. That's the clever bit, because when I came to I reckoned it was blood pressure or something through me changing the wheel. That's the *only* time anyone could have got 'em from me.'

'For God's sake, got what?' I said, acting like mad.

He studied me very closely and frowned. 'Who's in this with you?'

'I'm not in anything. And if you don't go this instant I'll call the police.'

'Go on then! Call the police!'

I went to the recess which housed the telephone and lifted the receiver. Of course this was what he wanted: to know where it was. With surprising agility he almost sprang across the room and, grasping the flex, wrenched it from the small black covering on the wall. I was still clutching the handpiece, and for the first time I can remember I was sufficiently annoyed to offer physical violence without considering the possible consequences.

I swung the handset round and hit him in the face with it. Sheer chance directed this at his left eye. He clapped a hand over it and staggered back and, rather half-heartedly this time, I hit him somewhere round his ear with my clenched fist. It was probably the fact that he was off balance that made him fall because I didn't strike him all that hard. On his way down he made a vain attempt to grab a chair, slid off it and bounced straight into the fireplace.

I let the handset drop and, standing over his spread-eagled figure, waited for him to get up. But he didn't get up.

I was breathing heavily now, as much from my un-characteristically violent emotions as from my exertions. Then slowly I realized that he wasn't going to get up. I stooped over him and saw that a trickle of blood was coming from his head. His mouth was half open and his eyes were in a fixed stare.

Rather pointlessly I said, 'Mr Cunningham! Mr Cunningham!' But Mr Cunningham didn't move. I dropped on my knees and touched him. 'Mr Cunningham!' Blood oozing from a wound at one side of his head was spreading across the fireplace and I could see what had caused it. A heavy fire-iron with a rather jagged edge also had a smear of blood on it.

To my credit, I didn't panic. A sort of cold, detached fatalism spread over me and I was conscious that every-thing was very quiet. I felt his pulse. Nothing! I felt his heart. Nothing! Then I dragged him so that he was lying flat on the fireside rug and began massaging his heart area. But I knew it was no good. He must have gone down pretty heavily on that fire-iron and the effect had been the same as if someone had struck him with the pointed end of an axe.

The blood was making a mess, so I hurried into the kitchen and got a couple of towels to pad round the wound. I poured myself a stiff whisky.

I suppose I should have called a doctor, and I would have done if I hadn't been quite sure he was dead.

When I had finished my whisky I went out to see where Cunningham's car was and found it parked in the road near my front gate. Then I hurried to a call box in the village and dialled Hannaford's number. Sally answered.

'Is Tom in?'

'I'm expecting him. You might find him at the shop. How's my portrait?'

'The portrait?' To hell with the portrait, I thought but I couldn't say that to her. 'I'm not yet satisfied with it.'

'Of course not. It'll take a long time, won't it?'

'To save me looking it up, what's the shop number?'

She gave it to me and said, 'I think he might be going away again next week.'

'Good,' I said but there must have been a certain lack of enthusiasm in my voice.

'You sound different,' she said. 'Anything wrong?'

'No, of course not. I want to catch Tom before he leaves. See you, Sally! Explain later.'

I put the phone down and rang the shop. Chapman answered at first and then Hannaford came on the line.

'Tom! I can't say much. I need you here as soon as possible.'

'By the sound of you, you do,' he said. 'I'll be down when I've squared up a few things here. I won't be long.'

'I rang your home first, so Sally knows I wanted to contact you.'

'I see. Thanks for telling me.'

It would take him half an hour to get to my place so I didn't hurry back. I wasn't over-anxious to hang about indoors with a dead man lying on the floor.

When I got near the house I saw his car and, stupid as it was, I couldn't help feeling a sort of sympathy for it, waiting for its master who would never come. I stopped when I got to it and, with nothing better to do, peered all round it. It was the blue Audi he'd had before, fairly new and well cared for. The inside looked inviting, upholstered in a lighter shade of blue. A packet of cigarettes was on the back seat and, on the front ledge, a pair of sunglasses. He had – or he *had* had – a flashy taste in headlights, with two rather pretentious extras fitted to the front bumper.

I went into the garden and mooched about. A good half-hour must have gone by since I'd telephoned, but I hadn't even considered what could be done. Until Hannaford arrived I had automatically opted out, as it were. But the sound of his car sliding up to the house quickened my senses. I went to the gate as he got out and saw him stare inside Cunningham's car.

'He's here, is he?' he asked.

'He's here. And he's dead!'

Most people would have said something at that, but all he did was to glance at me sharply and nod. Then we went in.

I don't know what I expected. In my youth I'd read corny detective stories where dead bodies mysteriously disappeared, and subconsciously I must have hoped for that to happen in this case. But the late Mr Cunningham was still there.

Hannaford stared down at him and his eye traced a line to the fire-iron.

'How long's he been like that?' he asked.

'About an hour.'

'Can't leave him much longer, then. He'll be getting difficult to move. What happened?'

I sank into a chair and explained everything. When I'd finished he went to the telephone and examined the wires.

'If you take off the cover you can screw these back,' he said. 'Can you manage that?'

'I expect so.'

'Right.'

He took off his jacket and, kneeling by Cunningham's body, felt his pulse. He lifted an arm and let it drop. Then he went through the pockets. Among other things, he found a folded piece of paper which he handed to me.

'Better burn that.'

In a neat back-hand was my name and address. I took the paper into the kitchen, put a match to it in the sink and washed the ashes down the drainaway.

When I went back he was missing, and I was about to start to look for him when he came from the hall carrying the tarpaulin which he had used to protect his car seat from our wet clothing the day I'd first met him. This he spread

out on the floor alongside Cunningham and rolled the
body on to it. Then he wrapped the tarpaulin round it
and stood up.

'What now?' I said.

'I'm going to back his car on to your drive and put
him in the boot. You have a look to see if anyone's about
and give me the tip-off if it's clear.'

He stood near the front door as I went to the gate and
when I called 'Okay!' he came down the path with
Cunningham's keys in his hand. Very casually he got
into the Audi and started the engine. Then with the
minimum of throttle he reversed the car on to the drive
where it was practically hidden from the road. He got
out and lifted the boot cover.

'Stay around, John, in case someone comes along,' he
said and he went indoors.

I stood near the front gate. A car went by at a fair
speed and droned away.

'All clear?' he called and, turning, I saw that he was
carrying the sagging, tarpaulin-covered body in his arms.
He held it in front of him as one would carry a baby.
Like that it must have been a weight, but he didn't seem
to notice it.

'All clear,' I said.

Rather more briskly he strode to the Audi and lowered
the body into the boot, easing it and forcing it until there
was nothing protruding. Then he shut the lid, locked it
and beckoned with his head for us to go into the house.

Inside he sat down and looked at me, his face very
serious.

'I got you into this and from now on it's my problem.
Leave everything else to me. Get in your car and drive
off somewhere and don't come back for at least three hours.
Is there anywhere you might have gone if this hadn't
happened?'

'Nowhere in particular. But I can't let you handle this on your own.'

'You've got to. Believe me, you won't be helping by getting further involved. He was obviously going to flog the stuff much sooner than I expected. It was a faint possibility and that's why I wanted to make sure there was no evidence to connect you with him.'

'There was. He recognized me.'

'So he did, but he would never have gone to the police.'

'How on earth did he find me?'

'He was no fool. He might have asked around various districts one at a time, Or he might even have got round some clerk in your bank and giving the address, or perhaps only the area where you live, wouldn't seem a very serious matter – particularly if a tenner changed hands! However, he did find you. Now he's dead and there's work to do. Why don't you get your equipment and drive down to Copley and paint the church or the old water-mill there? Have another go at an original.'

'I don't like it.'

'Hell, man, this isn't the time to argue. For the record, you left an hour ago. When you come back you will find that your rear door has been forced. You look round but there is nothing missing. You get rid of that rug he was lying on and those towels and clean up the bloodstains. Make a really good job of that. Mend the phone and then call the police. As nothing has been stolen, they won't bother with it much.'

'What are you going to do?'

'I'm going to drive his car to a place I know and leave it there. When it's dark, I'll return and, with him sitting in the driving seat, it will run down a bank into a tree.'

'What about your car? Who's driving that?'

'I will. I'll come back for it when I've placed his car where I want it. I'll get a train or a bus back to Felling-

bridge and walk the rest. It's only three miles away.
By the time you get back it'll be gone.

'Now, for my sake, stick to your story whatever happens.
You left an hour ago, went to Copley and painted whatever
it is. You came back and what happened in between you
don't know anything about. And you haven't seen me.'

I shrugged. I hadn't any ideas myself so I had no case
to argue. Collecting my things, I put them in the back
of the car and, as I was about to drive off, Hannaford
said, 'Don't have any qualms about Cunningham. He
should have been done in a long time ago!'

For the first few miles I drove automatically, my mind
in a state of suspension. I didn't really feel anything.
It was, I suppose, a biological antidote for shock which
had purged me of emotion so that I was able to remain
aloof from it all, at least for the time being.

When I reached Copley I found a quiet spot by the
mill, parked my car and, as if I had really intended doing
this all along and nothing untoward had happened back
there, I got out the equipment I needed. I set up my
easel and a frame and started work.

I kept at it for about an hour before the first of several
passers-by stopped and had a look. By now you could
at least see what it was intended to be but I knew that the
finished work wouldn't satisfy me. Trees have always
been my weak point and I'm not particularly clever with
cloud effects unless I'm copying. However, an elderly
man in a brown tweed jacket and slacks hovered a bit
longer than the others and eventually said, 'I see you've
got my cottage in.'

There were two cottages just to the left and behind
the old mill, which was the central feature. One was white
and one pink.

'Which is yours?' I asked.

'The pink one. Had it done last year for a change.
My wife would be interested in this. How much d'you

want for it when it's finished?'

I turned to have a better look at him. A pair of bushy, grey eyebrows were twisted in query and friendly, brown eyes in a lined, sunburned face regarded me with interest.

'I hadn't thought of selling it,' I said, 'and I don't know if it'll be good enough.'

He studied it again. 'It's coming on all right. Give me first offer, eh? Name's Armitage.' Then he grunted and moved off.

After that I put more emphasis on the cottages and an hour later the old chap passed by again on his return journey. 'I like it,' he said. 'Don't forget if you want to sell it!'

This broke my concentration and I realized that I'd had enough, so I packed up and drove off to find a pub for a drink and a snack.

I don't want to give the impression that I was completely insensitive to the previous events of the day or to what Hannaford was doing, but I had come to accept that it was his problem. He had, as he'd said, got me into it and, foolish though I may have been, I had been more sinned against than sinning. Such is the injustice of mental judgement when we are defending ourselves that I kept Sally out of the reckoning altogether.

It was on the way back home that I began to question Hannaford's reasons for the tortuous behaviour he had wanted of me, and particularly why I had to find my place broken into when I got back. But by the time I had pulled on to my driveway I had got no nearer reaching a rational conclusion. The fact that he undoubtedly had a reason was good enough, so I gave up and decided to carry out his instructions to the letter.

Both his and Cunningham's cars were gone and there was no outward sign that anything had happened. But sure enough, I found a pane of glass broken in the back door and the door open. I had a look round, checked that

everything was in order and turned to my next task:
the bloodstains. Here I challenged Hannaford's accepted
authority. It was a good rug, warmish brown in colour
and of the finest mohair. It would cost at least eighty
pounds to replace it. No, I thought, I'll see what it's like
when I've cleaned it. I took it into the kitchen and by the
time I'd finished I couldn't see a trace of blood anywhere.
The towels I wrapped in paper and set light to them in
the incinerator at the bottom of the garden.

After I had washed the fire-iron and all round the grate,
I replaced the rug and mended the telephone wires. Then
I rang the police. A woman switchboard operator put me
on to someone with a dark brown voice who said he'd
get one of the area cars along and advised me to make
absolutely sure nothing had been stolen and not to touch
anything.

About twenty minutes later I was letting in a uniformed
constable with a flat cap when I remembered that the
rug would still be damp, if not wet, and wondered if he'd
notice. Guilt can create non-existent problems in the
mind. But I needn't have worried. His general demeanour
suggested that he was due to go off duty and, as nothing
had been stolen, what was the point of his being there?

'You've had a good look round, have you, sir?'

'I certainly have. There's nothing missing and no sign
that anybody's been inside.'

'Perhaps you disturbed someone, sir, and they cleared
off before they had a chance to leave their mark.'

He was examining the broken glass and, watching
him, I thought he was very young and slender to carry the
responsibilities and physical risk of his calling.

'Was the door open when you got here?'

'Yes, but I know I locked it.'

'You shouldn't leave the key in. And a couple of bolts
would be more of a deterrent.'

'They'd find some way of getting in if they wanted to, wouldn't they?'

'Only if they thought it worth their while. For instance, if they knew you'd got several thousand quid stowed away somewhere or something really valuable. Have you?'

'No, nothing like that.'

'The casual breaker walks round looking for fanlights open or keys left in glass-panelled doors. If a place is reasonably secure he'll pass on to another one that's easier to get into. Sound the drum first, of course.'

'Sound the drum?'

'Make sure no one's in. Ring the bell and wait, especially at a place hidden away like this.'

'What about this glass?'

'You can clear it up, sir. Lock the door and take the key out. I know what you're thinking: fingerprints. As nothing has gone, we won't bother. He probably didn't touch it anyway and we've got too much to do. I'll just take a brief statement.'

When he'd finished, I asked him if he'd like a drink and, thinking back to the policemen in films, I expected him to say, 'No, thank you, sir, not on duty!'

But not a bit of it. 'That's very kind of you, sir,' he said.

'What's it to be?'

'Whisky, sir?'

I poured him a reasonable measure and, after a couple of mouthfuls, he started to reminisce.

'Talking about the casual breaker, about three years ago at Hemsford we had a really tough one to crack. Every Friday night this chap would do whole streets. Wherever he found an easy entry, he got in. No one heard him or saw him, and even dogs didn't seem to mind him. He only took cash, and sometimes from bedrooms where people were sleeping. Went through trouser and jacket pockets. This went on for months and it was making us look a lot of mugs. In the end we had special patrols out all night in plain clothes, hiding in alleyways and porches.' He tipped his glass again. 'Over a week we did this. I was one of them. Not very comfortable in bad weather, as it was, and dead boring. Anyway we caught him in the end.' He finished his drink. 'Turned out to be the son of a local magistrate! Thanks for the drink, sir. We'll be in touch if we nab anybody.'

I watched him go confidently down the path. Perhaps he wasn't so young after all.

My part was done, but the feeling of relief didn't last long. I began thinking of Hannaford and the far more difficult job he'd had to do, and I started to worry. Reaction was setting in at last.

Then the telephone rang and I found it difficult to breathe. I let it ring several times before I lifted the receiver.

Hannaford's voice came over. 'Tom here. How are you, John?'

'I'm okay. How are you?'

'You sound a bit off colour. I managed to get through a rather rushed programme today and I thought I'd relax now. What about a drink tomorrow?'

'Sure. Where?'

'The George at Wenstead would suit me best, as I'm staying in Town tonight. One o'clock in the saloon bar, okay?'

'Fine. See you then.'

That was all that passed between us but it was enough. We both knew that what had to be done had been done, but it didn't stop me wondering and worrying.

I'd never been in the George before, although I knew where it was. Wenstead, a fairly built-up area sprawled and fanned out from the end of a twelve-mile dual carriageway, and was heralded by a railway station and golf-course on one side and the George on the other.

It was a busy public house and hotel, much favoured by commercials, and at lunch-time you could go unnoticed unless someone was looking specifically for you.

I drew up in the spacious car park alongside a number of other vehicles and, as I shut off my engine, Hannaford appeared and slid in beside me.

'I parked near the entrance and waited for you to arrive,' he said. 'Thought we'd better have a chat before we go in.' He slid a mid-day paper from his jacket pocket and handed it to me, folded. 'There's one item in there you'd better read.'

It was about half way down in the centre, a three-inch column headed, BODY FOUND IN WRECKED CAR.

Last night the body of a man was found in a car which had left the road at Whittingham Gorge and had plunged nearly two hundred feet down the east bank where it crashed into trees below. The car was extensively damaged. The whole of the front had been telescoped and forced into the passenger compartment, the steering-wheel being crushed against the driver's chest. The driver is not being named until relatives have been traced. At this stage the police believe it was an accident but they have not entirely ruled out foul play.

I handed back the paper. 'Did he have any relatives?'

'A brother somewhere he hadn't seen for years. He was living with his fifth concubine and I don't suppose she'll be too upset.'

'So you managed it?'

'No trouble at all. I drove off the road first where I couldn't be seen, locked the car and left it. I went back and picked up my own car from your place and went to the shop. When it was getting dark I returned to Cunningham's car, transferred him to the driving seat and then let it go. I was about a hundred yards away when I heard the crash. After that I drove up to Town and stayed there. What about you?'

I told him what had happened and he nodded approval.

'The police will most probably accept it as an accident. If they don't, and if by some sheer fluke they find out he'd been to see you or somebody by your name, stick to your story. You've never seen him, ever. You went to Copley and when you got back you found your place broken into. Whatever they come up with, stick to it and don't enlarge on it.'

'But . . .'

'Trust me, John. You're not to get involved. If it looks like getting sticky, I'll sort it out. Remember! You've never seen him! Anyway, that's probably the last we shall hear of it.'

'Wait a minute,' I said. 'Suppose they find out I went to a house you rented and met him there?'

'They won't. Somebody rented it in your name, or it was somebody with the same name as you. No one saw you except Cunningham and he's dead. The ambulance men saw me but I didn't tell them who I was and I don't look much like you.'

'Did the bloke you rented the house from see you?'

'Only once when I took over and paid him. But he wouldn't recognize me now. The important thing for you to get firmly stuck in your mind is that you've never seen Cunningham here, there or anywhere.'

I didn't like it. Everything seemed to have become a tangled web of deceit and conspiracy. Whatever the original motives, it had all backfired. If it hadn't been for Hannaford I think I should have gone to the police with the whole story.

He jabbed me with his elbow. 'Come on, let's have a

drink. In a couple of months you'll have forgotten all about it.'

Events were to prove just how wrong even he, the expert planner, could be.

CHAPTER VIII

For three days nothing happened, nothing, that is, of any note.

On reflection that's not quite right. Something *did* happen to *me*. I discovered that my physical desire for Sally had faded. Once or twice I got out the portrait and added a few touches, but I lacked enthusiasm and each time I put it away within half an hour.

Occasionally I was haunted by the memory of Cunningham's sightless eyes staring up at me from the sitting-room floor, and there had been moments when I seriously considered selling up and moving somewhere else. But I overcame this feeling. I liked the place too much.

Each morning and evening I spent at the Stag and sometimes I had more than my usual quota of alcohol, including a few shorts which I normally drink only at home or when visiting friends.

One evening I must have let myself go a bit, because I began to notice that the regulars were treating me with less reserve. I suppose this was how the subject of Sally's previous visits to the cottage was brought up. Tony Sopwith started it. 'John,' he said, 'how's that tasty model of yours? You still painting her portrait?'

Being reasonably mellow, I remained unruffled. 'Not finished yet,' I said.

'Sure you're only painting her?' came from someone else.

I glanced at the speaker and by way of reply closed one

eye, something I would never have done at one time.
There were some amused chuckles and Sopwith said, 'I
reckon you ought to bring her in and introduce us.' The
others voiced their approval of this idea and I took the
easy way out. 'I might do that,' I said, 'as long as you
promise to behave yourselves.'

During the stroll home I felt a sudden urge to get away
for a while, somewhere abroad perhaps. Italy? Lake
Como? I'd been there before. Or France? Along the
Loire Valley? However, these ideas I discarded for the
time being when I saw the rear of Hannaford's car poking
from the cottage drive-in. Hannaford was standing with
his hands in his trouser pockets a few feet from the front
door, as if he had just rung the bell.

When he heard me, he turned and, still with his hands
in his pockets, came slowly along the path to meet me.
It took me only a few seconds to sense that this was an
entirely different Hannaford, one I'd never seen before.
His face had lost all trace of the calm, whimsical confidence
I had come to know so well. It was profoundly serious, his
eyes sharp but with an uncertain, worried look about them.
His shoulders drooped slightly too.

I stared at him and said, 'Hallo, Tom! Anything wrong?'

'Yes,' he said and my stomach lurched as I thought of
possibilities connected with Cunningham.

I opened the door and he waited until we were inside
before he enlightened me.

'Have you seen or heard anything of Sally during the
last few days? She's missing.'

'You mean?' I said, rather breathlessly. 'You mean
she's cleared off?'

'I mean she's missing. The last time I saw her was on
the morning of the day you rang me about Cunningham.'

I felt guilt suffuse me and covered it as best I could.

'I'm dreadfully sorry. Is there anything I can do?'

'You sure you haven't heard from her?'

'I spoke to her when I tried to get you on the phone about Cunningham. She said you might be at the shop and that's where I got you.'

'So she must have been there then.' He fell back into a chair. 'I could do with a drink.'

I hastened to get him one and, despite my session in the Stag, needed one myself.

'Have you had a row or anything?'

'No.'

'Did she leave any clue?'

'No.'

'Haven't you any idea where or who she might have gone to?'

'I thought she might have come to you. That was my best bet. I was giving it a couple of days.'

I didn't like the sound of that and I turned towards the window so that he couldn't see my face.

'Me? If she'd come here I'd have let you know.'

'Maybe. Sit down, John, and let's stop sparring. I know she's been coming here regularly when I've been away.'

Very slowly I took a drink from my glass as I tried to think. Then I sat facing him, feeling almost immune now from further shock. 'You knew? How?'

'She told me.'

'I was painting her portrait. It's out there.'

'I know. I've seen it.'

He looked away as he said this, so he didn't see the surprise and embarrassment which must have shown on my face.

'She told me about that too,' he said, 'and after you'd left for Copley I went into your studio and found it.'

A heavy silence hung between us. I wasn't going to

commit myself. Then, after a few sips at his glass, he raised his head and surveyed me with a rather sorrowful expression.

'You don't have to hedge with me,' he said. 'For one thing, I think too much of you. She knew that. Sexual love at its best is fine, but deep platonic affection between man and man, or man and woman for that matter, can transcend it. She also told me that the portrait idea was just a front to give you an excuse if ever I found out.'

'She . . . told you . . . that?'

He nodded and I passed a weary hand across my forehead.

'What did you say?'

'I told her not to raise you up to bring you down – not to hurt you. Where women are concerned you are oversensitive. You're a one-woman man while she lets it last.'

'You knew that too?'

'I guessed it after the first month or so of knowing you, which was why I contrived our evening out at the club. I gambled on the experience easing that side of you so that if – or rather when – she did start anything you'd be able to take it or leave it. I lost the bet.'

'Why did you introduce us then?'

'I didn't realize at first about this aspect of your character. And as we became such good friends, you'd have thought it odd if I'd never invited you to my place.'

'Why did she tell you?'

'Because she wanted to hurt me.'

'I don't understand it.'

'You don't have to. I'm not sure that I do myself. I'd better get on to the police. She's not here now, that's obvious.'

'Oh, my God! You think it's as bad as that?'

'As far as I can tell, she has nothing with her except the clothes she was wearing and no money to speak of. And her car's still in the garage.'

He lurched to his feet. Then he did a quite unexpected thing. He held out his hand and rather tentatively I took it. His grip became firm but not excessive.

'Leave it to me,' he said. 'None of this is your fault so don't blame yourself. Whatever happens I still regard you as a most sincere friend.'

I felt hollow inside. I could find nothing to say.

He let himself out and I heard his car drive away. Once again he had said, 'Leave it to me!' What else could I do?

For the next two days I lived in a state of uneasy truce between the warring of my conscience and what comforting logic I could muster, trying to forget some of the past and shutting my mind to the future.

It now seemed inevitable that the Hannaford period of my life would end as I suppose I had known it would. I thought often of Sally and conjectured a great deal, but it didn't get me anywhere. I pictured us both together, the look she would give me, our love-making. And I thought also of Hannaford as he had left me, the change in him and the things he had said.

I kept away from the Stag, going for long walks instead. I watched television in the evenings and I tried, without success, to read. I didn't sleep very well and by the fourth day I was beginning to feel the strain.

I had searched the newspapers – nothing! I'd had no word from Hannaford so I rang him. I rang at least six times without getting an answer and in the afternoon I drove to the shop.

Business seemed to be as usual, a few people looking round and a man and a woman discussing with Chapman the merits or otherwise of an antique writing-desk. There was no sign of Hannaford. The man bought the piece and seemed highly pleased.

Chapman, catching sight of me, came over. 'Afternoon,

Mr Bryant,' he said and stood beside me while he kept an eye on the shop. 'Have you seen Mr Hannaford today?'

'I was going to ask you the same thing.'

'It's two days since.'

'I haven't seen him for four days. That's why I called.' After I'd said it, I realized that he must have known it wasn't the only reason. Four days wasn't long when sometimes Hannaford would be away for weeks.

Chapman glanced at me quickly and cleared his throat. 'Did he say anything to you?'

'Yes,' I said and volunteered no more at this stage.

'Did he say anything about Mrs Hannaford?'

It seemed the time to quit stalling. 'Yes, he told me. He was going to the police.'

'He went to the police. I know that.'

'Is there anything else you know?'

A customer who needed attention interrupted our conversation and I had to wait until Chapman returned. 'He told me that the police took a description and other details, but they weren't yet treating it too seriously.'

'You mean they're doing nothing?'

'As I understand it, they'll circulate the description but apparently thousands of people walk out of their homes every year for no apparent reason. Most of them turn up eventually and get in touch.'

'But she didn't take anything – money, car or clothing.'

'According to them, that's not unusual either. Incidentally a police officer did call to see me but I couldn't tell him much.'

'I see.'

'If you want to know, I'm more concerned about him than her.'

It was my turn to glance at him and I waited for an explanation.

'He's not the same. Five years I've known him, since

I've managed this shop for him. He's not the same man at all.'

'Only to be expected.'

'I don't mean that. Naturally he's worried, but you know what he's like. He'd never let anything get him down. Before he left me he told me to cut prices and get rid of as much as possible.'

This I didn't like. 'Did he give a reason?'

'He said he was going to make some changes. Wouldn't tell me what. Frankly, I'm worried.'

'What's on your mind?'

'I think he's half decided to close up here.'

'Half decided? I've never known him "half decide" anything.'

'I said I thought he'd changed. You may think it's because if this place does close I'll be out of a job, but there's more to it than that as far as I'm concerned. I shall miss it. I love it. And there's him. He's the sort you'd do anything for. I'll miss him most. Even though he wasn't here a lot, I knew it was for him.'

'Yes,' I said 'I see what you mean.'

I got home about four, put the car away and cut the lawn. I was still in the garden when a voice from the side gate said, 'Good afternoon, sir,' and a man I'd never seen before came along the flagstone path towards me. He was sturdy and just under six feet I'd say, fair-haired and with a ruddy, open face. Friendliness and goodwill emanated from his pale blue eyes and even his gingery tweed jacket and trousers had a casual and homely appearance.

'Good afternoon,' I said, thinking perhaps that he was visiting some farm and had lost his way. But his next remark dispelled this idea. 'Mr Bryant?'

'Yes, that's right.'

He did a sleight of hand and produced a card which he held out for me to read. It was a police warrant card bearing his photograph which, although recognizable, made him look more like a frightened criminal than an officer of the law.

'Detective-Constable Hockett, sir.'

Remembering that Chapman had told me the police had been to see him, I assumed that this call was to do with Sally's disappearance.

'What can I do for you?'

'Before we have a chat,' he said, running a finger round the inside of his collar, 'd'you think you could let me have a drink of water. I feel absolutely parched.'

'Of course. I think I've got some orange squash in the refrigerator.'

'No, water'll be fine.'

He followed me into the kitchen and although he may have been genuinely thirsty I guessed afterwards that it was really an astute and tactful way of getting into the house. I filled a tumbler and put some ice in it, and he finished it off with a satisfied sigh.

'Thank you very much, sir. Now . . .' The progression to the sitting-room seemed perfectly natural. 'What I wanted to ask you was . . .' He felt in his inside jacket pocket. 'Do you ever remember seeing this man?'

Here he produced a photograph and thrust it towards me. I had to keep a grip on myself as I looked at it, for a very good likeness of Cunningham stared back at me. Frowning at it helped to hide my consternation and I pursed my lips to keep them from trembling. Then, shaking my head, I said, 'No. Should I have done?'

'That's another question. But you've answered the first one.'

One thing I noticed about him was that he didn't seem openly curious about the house itself. Whatever he observed – and observe he did – he wasn't obvious about it.

'How do you mean, that's another question?'

'Whether you should have seen him. Did you ever reside at or temporarily occupy an address known as The Beeches, Long Lane, Marchester?'

I was ready for it now. 'Never heard of the place.'

'You *are* Mr John Bryant?'

'Yes. Look, Officer, I don't mind co-operating but I think I deserve an explanation. Who is this man and why connect him with me?'

The fact that he was only a detective-constable seemed to give me considerable confidence. How wrong one can be!

'Of course, sir. The name of this man is Cunningham. He was involved a short while ago in a motor accident and was killed. From enquiries made, he appears to have visited a John Bryant who leased the property mentioned for a short time. Naturally, as that's your name we had to see you. No doubt it's another John Bryant somewhere, but we'll find him.'

'Have you a description of my namesake?'

'Not as yet, sir. Maybe it will come.' He shrugged his shoulders. 'Not to worry. And I must thank you for taking it so kindly. I'll be on my way.'

I followed him to the door but before he left I said, 'Why do you want to trace this other Bryant?'

He gave a slow, disapproving smile. 'As you're not him, I can hardly tell you that, can I, sir?'

'No,' I said, 'of course you can't.'

When he had gone, I sat quietly reassessing the situation, and one thing stuck out a mile. They wouldn't find another John Bryant who had had dealings with the late Mr Cunningham. Would they get back to me? And if they did, why? Another thing emerged from my contemplation: I needed Hannaford more than ever. I tried to ring his home again and again, and eventually in desperation I drove the fifteen miles to his place.

Before I rang the bell I knew there was no one inside.
Odd how an unoccupied house advertises that fact. I
went round to the back to signs of neglect. The lawn needed
cutting, the path sweeping and the greenhouse, with open
doors and fanlights, was a wilderness.

I returned to the car and waited. For over an hour
I sat, smoking and listening to the radio. I was on the
point of giving up when some inner instinct prompted
me to hang on a bit longer.

An interesting discussion on the merits of the work
of a well-known author who had recently died came to an
end and I re-tuned through several stations transmitting
either ghastly music of the mindless, repetitive variety or
sombre dirges I neither liked nor understood. So I switched
off. I was about to give up and had already turned the
ignition key when Hannaford's car slid on to the drive past
my own. I naturally expected him to see me but it was
soon obvious that he hadn't. He got out and, without
looking back, slouched to his front door. He was putting
the key in the lock when, now out of my car, I called,
'Tom!'

Lethargically he turned as if, whoever it was, it didn't
matter, and when I reached him I saw that there was mud
on his shoes and bits of grass, and a few short twigs' were
clinging to his crumpled trousers.

He said, 'Hallo, John!' and opened the door. Inside, he
threw his jacket in the direction of a chair without bothering to see where it landed and went straight to the cabinet.
He poured himself a huge whisky and drank a quarter of
it before pouring one for me.

Seeing him like this, I hesitated to mention my troubles
and the reason for my visit, so I sank into a chair and said
nothing.

He drank again, just a sip this time. 'I've been searching
for her,' he said.

'And you haven't found her?'

He shook his head. 'She could be anywhere.' He looked
directly at me. 'She's dead, John. I know.'

'I understand you've been to the police.'

'Where did you hear that?'

'Chapman told me. I've been worried about you.
Tried to ring you a number of times and couldn't get
you.'

'I went to the police. Missing persons? They can only
do the routine stuff until there's more evidence to support
my theory. Unfortunately I couldn't tell them everything.'

'What do you mean by that?'

'Never mind. How have things been with you?'

I told him about the visit from the police. He stroked
his chin thoughtfully and sat down.

'The last time I was at your place,' he said, 'I was too
worried to take it all in, but now I can remember that
the rug was still there. You didn't get rid of it, did you?'

'No. I washed it thoroughly. Do you think I should
get rid of it now?'

He shook his head vehemently. 'It's too late. Whatever
you do, leave it. I have a feeling about this. If they come
back, and I think they might, stick to your story. Promise
me that!'

'Yes, but . . .'

'I'm not going to explain. If you go against my advice
you'll be charged. Stick it out and however black it
seems you'll be in the clear. It's in your interest.'

I felt somewhat deflated, but he had more than enough
on his plate without having to worry unnecessarily over
me. I had an idea too that he wanted to be alone, so I
finished my drink and stood up.

'Is there anything I can do about Sally?'

'There's nothing.'

I left as he was pouring another drink.

*

That evening I got as near to being totally drunk as makes no difference. And it was at the Stag.

I was conscious of what was happening and as long as I didn't try to jerk my head suddenly or turn quickly I was able to move about with reasonable dignity. Or at least I thought I could. I was like two men: one, talking, making faces, arguing, laughing sometimes, and the other, standing outside the first and listening and making mental notes of it all. Both had one thing in common: a lack of restraint and inhibition. The man standing outside knew that the regulars in the bar were surprised, amused and taking advantage, but he didn't care. In fact in a masochistic sort of way he enjoyed it. Sooner or later someone brought up the business of Sally and her portrait. When were they going to see her?

'Come on, John, what about it?'

'I don't believe there is a portrait.'

Laughter . . . and so on.

I surveyed them in turn with what must have been a ponderous and absurd expression of wounded pride. That they should have doubted my word!

'All right,' I said. 'All right. All right. All right.' I kept on saying 'All right' until sudden inspiration jerked the needle free. 'If you don't believe me, come back. Have a drink. Will show you portrait. Okay? Okay? Okay?'

I'd never invited any of them to my cottage before and several of them immediately took me up on it. I think there were four, may have been five. I know Reg Smailes was one and Tony Sopwith another. I believe a chap named Barnard came too, but I can't remember who the others were.

We marched down the road with me sedately at the head, focussing on a distant object to keep to a reasonably straight line. When we reached my lane I steeled myself to turn slowly and immediately took my sights on the cottage. Then we were inside and I was pouring drinks and slopping some about as I handed the glasses round.

There was a lot of talking and laughter, and I can recollect stumbling through to my studio and returning with the portrait which, with a triumphant flourish, I placed on a chair.

I haven't the slightest idea what happened after that, for I awoke in the morning to bright sunshine, fully clothed except for my jacket, tie and shoes, and stretched out on my bed.

For a few minutes I stared at the ceiling and felt dizzy when I raised my head. I waited for an odd throbbing nausea to fade away, and then I saw that Sally's portrait was propped against the bedhead beside me. I must have remained remarkably still during the night or I should have knocked it to the floor. Looped over the top of the portrait was a sheet of paper on which was scrawled, 'You're okay, John. We believed you all along. Thanks for the drinks.'

It took me some time before I came round sufficiently to look at the clock. It was half past eight. I had a glass of Eno's, stripped off and had a shower and a shave, by which time I was more myself again.

I made some tea and toast, collected the morning paper from the doormat and sat idly turning the pages while I digested my breakfast.

Then it hit me, and I sat rigid as I stared at a photograph on the centre page. It was Sally, immediately recognizable, and I felt the bile come into my throat. She had been found among bracken on a lonely path by a man and woman walking their dog late the previous evening, at the same time perhaps that I was displaying her portrait to my drinking companions! The macabre aspect of that struck me as much as anything.

The place where she had been found was Copley and she had been strangled.

Every ten minutes for an hour I rang Hannaford's
number, although I felt sure he wouldn't be there. I
rang Chapman at the shop and he sounded shattered.
'Everything's happening at once,' he said, 'everything!'
He hadn't seen Hannaford nor heard from him. He didn't
know what to do except keep going as long as he could.

I now seemed to have reached a dead end. 'Dead' was
the operative word. Within the space of a few days a dead
man had been stretched out on my hearthrug and the
wife of a very good friend, a woman I'd made love to and
thought I loved, had been murdered.

I would have to get away – anywhere but miles away –
and try and resume the comparatively uneventful life
before I'd met Hannaford. I didn't think I'd have much
trouble in selling the cottage. If necessary I'd drop a little
on it to make a quick sale.

Whatever I might or might not have done in this respect
was for the time being ruled out, for shortly after eleven I
had another visit from the police.

I opened the door and facing me was a tall, dis-
tinguished-looking man in a grey suit. His hair was grey
and his well-balanced features and general air had the
stamp of authority. Just behind him stood Hockett, the
detective who had called before.

'Detective Chief Superintendent Anders,' said the man
in grey. 'Mr John Bryant?'

'Yes?' At this stage I wasn't unduly disturbed although
I was surprised and curious. Then I remembered Hannaford saying, 'They'll probably be back.'

'I believe you've met Detective Hockett?'

'Yes. He called the other day. Is there something
more?'

'May we come in?'

'Of course.' I stood aside and led them through into
the sitting-room.

Anders glanced at the newspaper which I had left

folded back to the page with Sally's photograph. 'I see
you've read the news about Mrs Hannaford.'

I picked up the paper, still not associating their visit
with her. 'Came as a dreadful shock. I knew her well.'

'That's one of the things we've come about. Naturally
we're making extensive enquiries into her murder and that
includes interviewing everybody who knew her.' He
looked meaningly at a chair and I made the appropriate
gestures. We all sat down and Hockett, still apparently very
friendly, gazed at me like a kindly welfare officer.

'How well did you know her?' Anders asked.

'She was a friend and so was her husband. I saw more
of him than her.'

He inclined his head very slightly. 'Would you say that
during the past few months that's quite true?'

'Well, yes. I was more his friend, you see. I mean . . .'

'Didn't she call here regularly when her husband was
away? Weren't you painting her portrait?'

'How did you know that? Did her husband tell you?'

'We've interviewed her husband and shall do so again.
He didn't mention you at all, a fact which I find rather
strange as we asked him to list all the people she knew.'

'I can't understand that either. But who told you about
the portrait?'

'Who else knew about it? I'd like to see it, if I may.'

I got it for him and for some time he held it at arm's
length and studied it. Then he stood it against a chair and
surveyed it from a distance. When he resumed his seat his
look was more calculating than before.

'I'm not an art expert by any means. I don't even know
whether that's good or bad, but you've put something into
it, something that doesn't come out in a photograph, and
I've seen a few of her.'

Whatever he meant by this more or less inconsequential
remark was lost on me at the time and his next question
and change of tone caused me to forget it.

'How much were you charging for the portrait?'

'Is that necessary?'

'Is it embarrassing for you to answer?'

'No, not exactly. I don't usually paint for money. This was for a friend. I wasn't charging anything.'

'How many sittings were there?'

'I don't know. Five or six. I didn't keep count. And I made a number of false starts.'

'What do you mean by that?'

'I couldn't get it right and had to paint it out until it came.'

'That perhaps was convenient?'

'Convenient?'

'Mr Bryant, I have reason to believe that you and Mrs Hannaford were lovers. I'm not moralizing but I'd advise you not to withhold anything from me.'

'What do you mean by "reason"?'

'On the twenty-ninth of July an officer called to see you about a car accident Mr Hannaford had and of which you were a witness. Before he left, a woman he has since identified as Mrs Hannaford came downstairs. You weren't painting her portrait then. I'll be frank with you. We also had two telephone calls, one we think from this village, informing us about the portrait you were painting of her.'

'You think it was from this village?'

'The caller wouldn't give his name and address and neither would the other caller who said that you and she had been lovers and that you had gone to Copley the day she was murdered. Well, Mr Bryant, I've laid a few of my cards on the table.'

I felt like a fish that had taken a bite and just couldn't get away in time. Anders, the expert angler who had seen the float bob, jerked the line.

'How many times did she call on her own to see you before the portrait was suggested?'

TO DIE A LITTLE

I suppose I could have told him to go to hell. I was ashamed now of what I'd done, or been led to do, but it had been no crime and Hannaford, the really injured party, knew and had forgiven. Yet I felt obliged to answer.

'Three or four. I can't remember exactly.'

'You made love then?'

'After the first time.'

'When did you last see her?'

I thought back and gave him a date I reckoned was about right.

'Are you sure it wasn't on the tenth of August?'

'Of course I'm sure.'

'On that day what did you do?'

As memory clarified I felt sweat beads beginning to form. It was the day Cunningham had called, the day he had been killed. I knew what I had to say.

'In the afternoon I went to Copley and painted the old mill. I've got it here.'

'Can I see it?'

Once more I went into the studio and came out with the painting. He looked at it.

'And you say that Mrs Hannaford didn't go with you?'

'Of course she didn't. I told you when I last saw her.'

'We believe that she died on or about that day. And, as you know, she was found at Copley. It is a coincidence, isn't it?'

He didn't say it in a sneering, sarcastic way but at that moment he seemed a very nasty man indeed.

'Are you trying to say you suspect me – *me* – of killing her?'

'Detective Hockett has already asked you if you are the Mr Bryant who had some connection with the late Mr Cunningham who, incidentally, was also murdered.'

'Murdered?'

'Let's say he was killed before the accident happened. That we *do* know. He was also killed on or about the tenth of August.'

'Look, I've had enough of this!'

'So have I, Mr Bryant.' Anders nodded to Hockett who took out a pocket book and held a Biro poised to write. They both stood up and, as if by some disciplinary command, I also stood up.

'John Bryant, I am arresting you on suspicion of murdering Sally Nicola Hannaford on or about the tenth of August. You needn't say anything, but anything you do say will be taken down in writing and may be given in evidence.' He turned his wrist. 'The time is eleven-thirty.'

'This is bloody madness,' I said. Everything was closing in on me. I felt myself swaying. 'I haven't murdered anybody.'

'We shall make a thorough, scientific examination of this house, your clothing and your car.'

I began to recover. 'Only with me present!'

'I'll agree to that naturally. But we'll take this rug with us now.'

CHAPTER IX

The car outside was a large white Granada. They put the rolled-up rug in the boot. Hockett drove and I sat in the back with Anders. As we turned out of my lane, I noticed with some surprise a few locals standing about in twos and threes along the road. They all showed consider-able interest in the car and it was patently obvious that they knew what was going on. It struck me then that here perhaps was the source of the police information about the portrait. One of them who had seen it had also seen Sally's photograph in the paper the following day.

'*Did* somebody from here tell you about the portrait?'
I asked.

Anders gave me a quick sidelong glance. 'As I said, it could have been.'

'They actually mentioned the portrait?'

'I should remind you that you have been cautioned. You were a possible suspect, and having questioned you I consider you a prime one. Therefore I have no other recourse but to take you in for further questioning and await the result of other enquiries.'

'I did *not* murder anybody.'

'You would hardly say otherwise, would you? I think it only fair to advise you that you have every right to call a solicitor when we get to murder headquarters at Copley.'

'Murder headquarters?' The term sent a shiver through me.

'Of course. Investigations have to be localized at first.' He seemed very casual and uncomfortably sure of himself.

'I don't need a solicitor. I haven't done anything.'

'Good for you! However, if you are charged I advise you to get one.'

'*If* I'm charged? I thought I was going to be.'

'Not necessarily. At the present time the evidence points to you but we may find other factors which throw a different light on it. Now I want to be perfectly fair with you. Unless you want to make a confession, say nothing more for the time being. I have enough on you to hold you as it is. Later on we'll see.'

I think I should have felt less uneasy if he hadn't been so damned gentlemanly about it all. Psychologically all this wanting-to-be-perfectly-fair stuff made me more nervous than I would have been. Perhaps he guessed that, had assessed my character and knew it was the best ploy.

For the rest of the journey I sat thinking. I was horrified

at the suggestion of even being associated with the cause of Sally's death, but I had a clear conscience about it. The Cunningham affair was different. I wasn't guilty in the true sense but I had been involved in his death, and I *was* withholding information from the police. How or why they linked the two I couldn't imagine.

It now seemed clear that Hannaford had anticipated possible difficulties over the Cunningham enquiry and, remembering his advice, I decided to stick to it. I owed him and myself that much. But how would he take the entirely different angle of my being arrested for his wife's murder?

Whatever the eventual outcome, by the time we reached Copley a sullen, brooding mood had enveloped me, so that when we pulled up outside a small, detached house and I was led inside, I ignored questions and remarks directed at me and refused a cup of tea brought to me in the small room where I was to all intents and purposes a prisoner.

Several hours went by, during which time I had at least three changes of policemen closeted with me. They were all uniformed but as I ignored them and refused to speak I couldn't say what they were like. Most of the time they sat near the door and read.

Hockett came in once and asked me what I wanted for a meal.

I said, 'Nothing.' I wasn't being difficult. I think I should have spewed it all up if I had tried to eat.

At my request a constable did show me to the lavatory, but I found it disconcerting when he put his foot in the door and insisted on it remaining there. Events had somewhat loosened my bowels but I have always found it embarrassing and difficult to perform the most natural of functions in anyone else's immediate presence. Somehow I managed although I didn't like it, and I returned with a feeling of humiliation. The constable seemed to regard it as routine.

Then Anders appeared with a very large man whom he introduced as Detective Chief Inspector Carver, and the uniformed constable in attendance went out.

I suppose in different circumstances I should have assessed Carver as a pleasant enough fellow as long as you didn't try anything physical with him. He was immaculately dressed, which contrasted a little with the pugilistic stamp of his features. However, as matters were, I liked him no more than I did Anders, and I suspected him also of playing me along until he was ready for the heavy stuff.

They sat down at the table and both pulled out pocket books and wrote something in them, after which they looked at me. I stared back defiantly and said, 'Well?'

'No, Mr Bryant,' said Anders, 'it is not well. Do you still maintain that you have never seen or had personal contact with the late Mr Cunningham?'

Whatever they come up with, Hannaford had said!

'Yes, I do. Why?'

'The rug we took from your house has been scientifically examined and we can now prove that small strands of hair from this were found on Cunningham's clothing. Furthermore, a speck of blood still remaining on the back of the carpet is of the same group as Cunningham's. Without doubt he was killed in your house.'

This was an unexpected and demoralizing stroke. I was sitting forward, my head lowered slightly, forearms resting on my knee. I remained perfectly still so I don't think they were able to read my face. Slowly I allowed the tension to drain out of me.

Whatever they come up with! Had Hannaford anticipated this? He'd told me to get rid of the rug. Then after Hockett had called, he'd advised me to leave it. I could see now that if it had been missing when Anders had arrived I could hardly have maintained ignorance of its significance. More than ever I was resolved to stick it out. I sat up and crossed my legs.

'I've already told you. I went to Copley and didn't get back until after nine. Then I found my place had been broken into and rang your people.'

'We have a record of that. You found nothing missing or disturbed, I believe?'

'That's right, but someone could have been inside. This Cunningham, dead or otherwise, wasn't there on the rug or anywhere else.'

'He wouldn't have been. About that time his body was in a car hurtling down a bank at Whittingham Gorge, which wouldn't be far out of your way home from Copley. Who washed the main bloodstains from the rug? The few traces we found couldn't have got under the pile by themselves.'

'I don't know. *You* tell me. Anyway, I thought I was supposed to have murdered Mrs Hannaford. Did I kill both on the same day?'

'Is that so unlikely? You had the opportunity and perhaps the motive.'

'I hadn't any motive.'

'Until this morning you weren't suspected of murdering Mrs Hannaford. We did, however, have reason to connect you with the death of Mr Cunningham. After many enquiries we traced only three John Bryants, including yourself, who could have been the one we were after. The other two we were able to rule out fairly quickly, and you were the only one who had a brown mohair rug in his house. Fibres from such a rug were, as I've said, found on his clothing. In his own flat Cunningham didn't have such a rug. We traced his movements before he reached your house. No brown mohair rugs anywhere. So we were looking for a John Bryant who had a brown mohair rug and we've found one. At least Detective Hockett did.'

Hockett! And he'd seemed such a nice chap!

'This is nonsense,' I said. 'Why would I want to kill him?'

'That we have to find out. He had been in your house and his blood was found on your rug. You denied that he'd been there. Almost certainly he was killed in your house. Being the owner and only occupant, you had the opportunity. You also had the opportunity to stage the so-called accident. We found correspondence from you to him and copies of letters from him to you.' He produced a letter which he held out for me to read. 'That's your signature, isn't it?'

It was the letter Hannaford had written and signed in my name.

'It looks like my signature but it isn't. I've never seen that letter before.'

He put it back in his folder and stared at me.

'This morning,' he said, 'we learned of your connection with Mrs Hannaford. We also found out you'd been to Copley at about the time of her death.'

I frowned at this but said nothing.

Suddenly in a louder, firmer and more commanding tone he said, 'Did you kill her, Mr Bryant?'

At this I hit my knee with my clenched fist and almost shouted, 'No, I bloody well didn't.'

Anders and Carver glanced at each other and some hidden message seemed to pass between them.

Then they stood up and Anders said, 'You will go with Mr Carver and other officers to your house where a search will be made. They will bring back all your clothes they consider necessary and these will be sent to the lab for examination. The outer clothes you have on will be examined, so before you go a temporary replacement will be provided for you.'

The whole thing seemed to be escalating out of all proportion to the indiscretions I had committed.

'I think you said I can call on a solicitor?'

'Yes, when we get back.'

'But someone could contact him for me while I'm gone. Tell him I want to see him.'

'All right. Who is it?'

'Mr Hannaford.'

There was a short silence.

'You mean Mr Hannaford, the husband of the murdered woman?'

'Yes.'

'I said "a solicitor".'

'He is a solicitor. He hasn't practised for some time but he's qualified.'

Another short silence.

'It's out of the question. Surely you can see that?'

'No, I can't. Unless *he* doesn't want to see me. He's a solicitor and the one I want to see.'

Anders sat down again and Carver, who so far hadn't spoken a word, said, 'I'll get things organized,' and left. Then Anders quietly studied me until I began to wonder what on earth was going through his mind. In a different situation his constant and prolonged gaze would have been decidedly rude. Then he stood up again. 'There's one thing,' he said. 'There'll be no trouble contacting him. He's with us now, also helping with our enquiries. I'll decide about it when you get back.'

A constable brought me a pair of slacks and a jacket which just about fitted, also several pairs of light shoes for me to choose from.

'How long am I supposed to wear these?' I asked.

'I can't say,' said the constable. He was a long, lean young man and he treated me with the cautious indifference of someone used to dealing with criminals who have for the time being been brought under control.

Each new experience was having the effect of depressing me further and challenging my resistance. Was this, I thought, why they did it? To hell with them!

We drove back to the cottage in the same Granada, followed by a blue van. This time Carver sat in the back with me. The driver I gathered was a Detective-Sergeant Bridge. When we arrived I let them in and two plain clothes men, one carrying a large black case, came in as well.

Carver and Bridge went over the place thoroughly. They took all my outer clothes and my shoes, and put them in the van. The two pictures which had interested Anders they didn't bother about.

Very little was said during this time, but, as the three of us passed through the sitting-room on the last occasion, one of the officers, who was in the process of sealing an envelope, pointed to the two fire-irons which were now resting on brown paper on the table.

'I think we'd better take these, sir,' he said to Carver.

The Chief Inspector turned to the sergeant. 'Go with Mr Bryant to the car,' he said. 'I'll be with you in a moment.'

Dumbfounded, I allowed myself to be ushered out by the sergeant and without a word got into the back of the car. I shook my head when he offered me a cigarette and sat glumly wondering what they could have found on the fire-iron. The bits of rug on Cunningham's clothes I had foolishly not considered, but I had washed that fire-iron thoroughly and wiped it.

I don't know how long I sat there and I was beginning to feel exhausted. My stomach was rumbling yet I still couldn't face the idea of food.

Then Carver was beside me again and we were driving back to that terrible place – or so I thought. But we didn't go to Copley. They took me instead to Police Headquarters at Hemsford, a large, modern building which I had seen before only from the outside. I had never dreamed that I would one day be an unwilling visitor and become involved in the mysteries within.

The car slid round the back and up to a door away from prying eyes, and I was led into what was obviously quite an extensive cell block. There were passages, iron grilled doors which clanged and intimidating background noises. I was taken to a small room which had walls faced with polished wood to take off the austerity, a small table, two chairs and a built-in divan along one side. There were a few books and colour supplements on the table and an ashtray. The ashtray was strangely comforting.

Carver followed me inside and stood near the door, his brows wrinkled and his strong face not unfriendly.

'I understand you haven't eaten since you've been with us?'

I sat on the edge of the divan. 'No.'

'I advise you to. Guilty or innocent, you need something. We can provide the usual fare for you or, if you want anything different, you can pay for it. We can take this from the money you had in your possession.'

'How long am I going to be here then?'

'That depends. For the night at least.'

'Anders, your superintendent, is doing his best to build up a black case against me.'

'He's doing nothing of the sort. He is acting according to the evidence available.' My remark seemed to have annoyed him. 'He's treated you very fairly, more than some I know would have done.'

'Is it fair to detain an innocent man?'

'If you *are* innocent, it's unfortunate. And if you are, we'll do our best to establish your innocence. As it is, it doesn't look that way, does it?'

'I don't care how it looks.'

'Unfortunately we have to, otherwise we'd never arrest anybody or solve anything. Now, what about this food?'

He was talking sense. I had underestimated the system and the men behind it. Although I wasn't going to admit it, I *had* seen Cunningham dead on my floor and deduction and science had brought the police in the shape of Hockett and Anders. Could I really blame them? Could I justifiably take exception to anything Anders had done? Certainly not in the case of Cunningham. But I hated the idea of being suspected of Sally's murder and it still needled me.

'I suppose I ought to eat,' I said. 'The way my inside's churning about, it had better be something light. Can someone get me a Dover sole and creamed potatoes?'

'I think we can manage that. Would you like some coffee?'

'Yes, please – black and no sugar.'

'I'll see what I can do.'

He hesitated at the door. 'You don't look like a man who would assault and murder a woman,' he said, and with that he went out and locked the door behind him.

It seemed rather pointed that he hadn't included, *and kill a man and dispose of his body*, but I must say his attitude and parting remarks did bring some comfort.

Therefore when a uniformed constable brought the meal I had ordered I was more prepared for it. He gave a brief nod, put the tray on the table and left. The key grated in the lock and the sound of his footsteps receded.

I ate it all and drank the coffee. Then I sat back with my legs up on the divan and smoked my pipe.

I did feel better. It had been stupid to go without food. The nervous system needs sustenance as much as the rest of the body. I began to think more clearly and one thing gradually emerged from my mental probing. I had trusted Hannaford too much. Okay, he hadn't killed Cunningham. He'd got rid of his body but he hadn't killed him. I'd done that even if it had been an accident. But what about Sally? If anybody had a motive, it was him. Perhaps the front he'd put up about not worrying over her visits to me had been a smokescreen and the attempts to find her just a convincing act.

Then it hit me forcibly. I'd told no one that I had been to Copley. He and I were the only ones who should have known, yet someone had rung the police and told them. Small incidents came back, merging together towards a meaningful conclusion, and it began to dawn on me that perhaps I had been casting Anders and his men in the wrong role. Maybe they weren't ruthless man-hunters out to make an arrest come what may. They could in fact turn out to be my saviours in the end. Even in my previously muddled state my dealings with them had proved them far from fools.

After I had been to the lavatory and had a wash, I felt better still. I saw by my watch, which they had left me, that it was gone nine. I flicked through the magazines and did half a crossword. Every now and again someone lifted the flap of the round peephole in the door and then went away.

At ten I undressed, put on the pyjamas and slipped between the sheets. Not unnaturally I couldn't sleep and about eleven I heard footsteps approach. I expected an eye at the peephole again, but this time the key turned in the lock and the door opened. It was Anders.

'I don't suppose I woke you?' he said.

'No, you didn't. What's happening now?'

'I felt you ought to know. As far as the murder of Mrs Hannaford is concerned, we wouldn't hold you. You have not been entirely ruled out as a suspect, but unless something else comes to light the evidence we have suggests you didn't do it.'

I reached for my pipe and pouch, and clumsily stuffed tobacco in the pipe bowl.

'Thanks for that anyway,' I said, puffing at a lighted match.

'Are you comfortable?'

'I'd be more comfortable at home.'

'I suppose you would. However, there's the matter of Cunningham. Would you care to say what happened?'

'I don't know what happened.'

He nodded as if he'd expected me to say that, but didn't believe me.

'Do you still want Mr Hannaford to act for you?'

My awakened awareness of the many sides of Hannaford caused me to make some rapid readjustment of the pros and cons. Then I decided.

'Yes, I want to see him.'

'In that case he'll be along in the morning.'

I slept fitfully, often waking and wondering where the hell I was, and then re-living the mess I'd got myself into until my eyelids drooped and I dozed off again.

At seven a constable came in and asked me if I was all right. He suggested I get myself ready for breakfast which would be along fairly soon. After a wash and a shave, I didn't feel too bad.

About eight o'clock the same constable appeared with a plate of fried egg, bacon and sausage, some bread and a small pot of tea. But it was the folded morning paper lying across the tray which surprised me.

'Do all prisoners get this attention?' I asked.

'Not quite,' he said. Then he glanced round the room and left without committing himself further.

It was true that now the possibility of being charged with Sally's murder had been lifted, or practically so, I felt quite different. I didn't resent the place so much. As long as my stay was to be relatively short, it was a unique experience so far as I was concerned.

It had been good of Anders to let me know. Or had it? I was beginning to have doubts about everything and everybody and, perhaps because of this, I had more confidence and a crafty belligerence which is normally quite foreign to me.

About nine the constable took away the tray. I had
finished scanning through the parts of the paper which
interested me when Anders arrived with the sergeant
who, with Carver, had brought me to the police station.

'Did you have a reasonable night?' asked Anders.

'Reasonable, yes. I have a clear conscience.'

He pulled a chair out, sat at the table and produced
his notebook and ballpoint pen. He wrote the date and
time and nodded at the chair opposite to him.

'D'you mind sitting there?'

I sat.

'I think I should remind you of the caution,' he said,
and he went over the same routine about the fact that I
needn't say anything. I always think this is an odd pro-
cedure because if you were innocent you'd want to say
plenty.

'In the first place,' he went on, 'one of your fire-irons
most probably killed Cunningham. The sharpish end fits
exactly the deep, penetrating wound that killed him.'

In my new mood I just looked at him with curiosity.

'I think it was the fire-iron on the right,' he continued,
'facing the fireplace.'

'That's very clever of you. Naturally I haven't the
faintest idea how he was killed, but how did you arrive at
that conclusion?'

'For two reasons. The fire-iron from the right had
been cleaned thoroughly as if it had been washed and
wiped. The other, although not dirty, was by no means so
clean.'

I almost gave myself away there. The things you fail
to think of! The fact that one was much cleaner was
probably noticeable in the crevices where a duster can't
reach.

'Also the bloodstains found on the base of the rug were

on the right, indicating that his head must have been at
that end some time. As it is a half-moon-shaped rug, with
only one straight edge, there is no question of it ever
having been in any other position.'

As if I were interested only from a purely academic
point of view, I nodded sagely but kept quiet.

After a pause, Anders said, 'Is there anything you want
to say now?'

I was impressed and a bit uneasy again but I managed
to cover it.

'There certainly is. From what you tell me, and I
congratulate you, it appears that this man *was* killed in
my house. But why do you keep on insisting that I had
anything to do with it? I went to Copley. I told you.'

'That proves nothing. We have checked the pub you
say you went to but no one remembers you there. You have
no corroboration as to the time you left home and when
you got back.'

'I don't need it.'

'There is the correspondence between you and Cunningham. We know that he was an unpleasant character.
If you hadn't cancelled your cheque, you would have lost
a hundred pounds, plus any more he conned out of you.'

It nearly caught me and I wondered if he had noticed
my hesitation.

'What cheque? I didn't write him a cheque,' I said, but
I knew I was playing with fire. There was a cheque. Had
he found it? Was he playing me on a long line?

'The cheque which matches the blank stub in your
cheque book. Your bank manager confirms that you
cancelled it by phone. He also says he received confirmation by letter from you, sent from an address in Marchester.
We have the letter.'

'If someone rang him it wasn't me, and I certainly
didn't write to him. If he did get a letter, someone must

have been impersonating me.'

Anders continued to look at me placidly.

'Where is the cheque – or the letter?' I said. 'Let me see them.'

He ignored the question. 'Going back to the fire-iron, Cunningham could have been struck with this but I don't think so. It would have been a clumsy weapon to get hold of and, from the position of the wound and the angle of entry, it would have had to be lifted fairly high. The ceiling in your room is low. My theory is that there was a struggle and he was struck or pushed so that he fell and, with his full weight behind it, his head met the fire-iron. There would not have been much blood at first. You dragged him on to the rug and later disposed of his body by staging the accident.'

'But I was at Copley painting.'

'So you said. I've seen the picture. But you could have painted that the day before or the day after.'

It came to me then. If I hadn't been so emotionally upset over Sally's murder I might have thought of it before.

'Wait a minute! Wait a minute! There *was* someone who saw me painting the old mill, an old boy who came by not long after I'd started and again about two hours later.'

Anders's gaze sharpened slightly. 'Can we trace him?'

'You should be able to. In the picture there are two cottages. His is the pink one. He got interested in what I was doing and said he might like to buy it when it was finished.'

'We'll check on this. It is our duty to do so.'

'You've got my keys. Go to my place and take the picture. You'll see the cottage I mean. Ask him if he remembers the incident and if he remembers how long I was there. Now, I'm not answering any more questions.

I thought I was to see Mr Hannaford this morning?'

He made a few entries in his book and the sergeant, who had been doing so on and off all the time, put his book away.

Anders stood up. 'Is there anything else you want?'

'Only to get out of here.'

'I'll see if Mr Hannaford has arrived.'

After they had gone, I sat for a while congratulating myself on one or two narrow escapes. I occupied myself with the newspaper again and re-read a follow-up item on Sally's murder: *A man who has been kept overnight at Police Headquarters, Hemsford, is helping the police with their enquiries.* There was another photograph of Sally and further details of her murder. Her death, the manner of it, and our former intimacy had produced scars which would remain for a long time, if not for ever.

Footsteps again! The door opened and there was Hannaford! The whimsical and lazy humour in his face was not there, but otherwise he looked the old, confident Hannaford.

The door shut behind him and we were alone. Immediately he put his finger to his lips and pushed a slip of paper at me. I took it and read: 'Careful what you say. Have you admitted anything? If not, shake your head.' I shook my head. 'Don't tell me any more than you've told the police. Leave the rest to me.'

Leave the rest to him! That's what I'd been doing all along.

He sat down. 'Well, John, it grieves me to see you here. Start from the beginning.'

I held his eyes very steadily. 'They suspected me of Sally's murder.'

'I heard about that. I never believed it for one moment.'

'They think now I'm clear of that but they suspect me of killing a man named Cunningham.'

'Tell me about it.'

I told him what had happened, carefully choosing my words so that anybody overhearing could not suspect any collusion between us.

When I'd finished, I said, 'I feel dreadful about Sally,' and when there was no reply, 'It must be terrible for you. I am deeply sorry.'

At that he lowered his head and very quietly said, 'Yes, it is.'

'One thing I don't understand,' I said. 'You and I were the only people who knew I had been to Copley that day. I told no one, yet the police knew. Someone got on the phone to them, someone who wouldn't give his name. Who do you think it might have been?'

Hannaford frowned. 'I'll look into that.'

'I understand they had you in for questioning?'

'It was a natural progression but I was able to clear myself to their satisfaction, or at least I think I was. I had to supply a good deal of background too.' He stood up. 'Now, say nothing and answer no questions. You'll be out of here before long.'

'You're going?'

'Yes. I have things to do.'

After that I had enough to think about. Over an hour went by. Somebody brought me coffee. Nearly another hour and Anders came in with Carver.

'We're going to release you,' said Anders. 'I'm not yet satisfied that you have been entirely truthful, but Mr Armitage, who owns the cottage at Copley, has corroborated your story and the times more or less correspond.'

'Thank God for that!'

'On the evidence we *now* have, I think it would be wrong to hold you, but I must ask you not to leave the district until I say. We also want your passport if you have one.'

'It's out of date but you can have it.'

'Your property will be returned to you and you will be taken home.'

Taken home! How marvellous that sounded, even though there was no one waiting to welcome me!

CHAPTER X

Hockett took me back and such was his personality that I allowed myself to be engaged in general conversation which, for tactical reasons no doubt, he steered well clear of the matter of my arrest and the causes for it. Nevertheless, I was careful. I had been bitten once by Mr Hockett! Not that I blamed him. It was his job and I sensed that basically he was a nice chap.

When we arrived, he stopped long enough to collect my passport and then he left. I went round the place quickly, returning to the sitting-room where the absence of the rug and the fire-irons stuck out at once. They had kept them and frankly I didn't want them back.

I tried to telephone Hannaford but he wasn't at home, or he refused to answer. Neither was he at the shop and Chapman seemed more concerned than ever.

'I'm worried about him, Mr Bryant. He hasn't been near and I'm selling stock fast. Word seems to have got round and I've hardly anything left.'

I wasn't all that concerned about Chapman's troubles although I did feel sorry for him. The least Hannaford could have done, I thought, was to give some reassurance to a loyal employee.

I went for a long walk in the afternoon and had what is normally referred to as 'high tea' in Brinkford, a small village that is reached via the towpath three miles down river.

In the evening I found myself brooding over the informer from the pub, and once the seed had been sown my resentment grew and grew until I knew I had to face it.

In the Stag there was the usual crowd plus one or two strangers. I don't think anyone saw me at first but when I drifted round to the bar and in a loud voice called out to George, 'A pint of mild, please,' the conversation stuttered almost to silence.

George drew off my beer and I slid over the right money. Then, with my drink in my hand, I pushed towards the middle of the bar counter and stood with my back against it. Two people who didn't know me from Adam were talking but when I said, 'It's nice to know who your friends are,' they stopped. I had the floor and I kept it.

'Someone here telephoned the police and told them I had been painting a portrait of Mrs Hannaford who was murdered the other day, and that she had been calling on me regularly, someone who hadn't the guts to give his name.' Then I lied. 'But I know who it was.' I glanced quickly at each of those who had seen the portrait. 'It was bad enough to find out that she had been killed without being unjustly accused of murdering her. For the information of the Judas who accepted my hospitality on one occasion, I have been completely cleared of any implication in the murder. But I spent a very uncomfortable twenty-four hours waiting for that to happen.'

There were a few murmurs of sympathy and heads shook. 'Don't know anything about it.' 'Not me.' 'We'd heard you'd been arrested and naturally thought they had something on you.' And so on. But by now I had a good idea who the informer was. Sopwith, whose face had given him away, slipped out quietly after he had finished his beer.

Reassurances came at me from all sides. No doubt some of them felt a prick of conscience for even thinking I might be guilty after the police had arrested me.

Frogget said, 'Well, who did phone the bloody police?'

'Only four of us saw the picture John painted.'

'It wasn't me.'

'Nor me. If I've got anything to say to anybody I'd let 'em know who was saying it.'

'What about whoever saw her for real when she called at John's place?' said George from behind the bar.

'That was Charlie, a couple of times, and he was more taken with her legs and tits than anything.'

I flushed at this crudity, tactless in the circumstances, and Charlie Stanford, who was there, said, 'I don't know about that but I wouldn't have recognized her again, and I certainly didn't do any phoning.'

'Where's Sopwith?' said Sam Kendrick. 'He was with us that night and he was here a short while ago.'

'He was here,' I said rather pointedly. 'He went out not long after I came in.'

There was an awkward silence which gave added emphasis to my statement and then, as if the matter had been shelved provisionally, I was plied with questions about my unpleasant experience. Drinks came regularly and by the time I set off for home it was getting dark and I was within a knife edge of being under the influence. I suppose I *was* to a degree under the influence. I could walk steadily, if rather ponderously, and I could think. But I felt I didn't care much what happened. Neither did I bother to notice things around me, and I reached the cottage more by instinct than any sense of direction.

As I pushed through the gate, I remember wondering who it was who had made the other phone call to the police, telling them I'd gone to Copley and, almost certainly, of my intimate relationship with Sally. Perhaps I had jumped the gun. Maybe nobody from the pub had telephoned. Perhaps someone else had made both calls. But I doubted it, especially having seen the expression on Sopwith's face before he left.

I was fumbling with my door key when it happened.

Something firm and heavy, but not hard, descended on the back of my head with considerable force, producing a stunning effect without putting me right out. I staggered and felt my knees sag, and before I could even start to recover someone had looped a rope over my shoulders and down, pulling it tight to pinion my arms. Again it went round and then I was pulled to the ground, face down. A hard knee went in my back and strong fingers deftly bound my wrists together. I was still trying to get out of the fog when I was blindfolded. Slowly I came to my full senses but I couldn't make any effective movement and I couldn't see.

'What's the bloody game?' I said. 'Who is it?'

A deep, gruff voice I didn't recognize – or did I? – said, 'Get up.'

'What if I don't?'

'If you don't, I'll kick you in the balls.'

I tried to place the tone, the accent and the manner of speech but, although there was still something familiar about it, I couldn't. As I wasn't all that keen on being kicked in the testicles – and from the treatment I'd already received I reckoned my unknown assailant would undoubtedly carry out his threat – I struggled to my knees and then to my feet.

'Do as I say,' said the voice, 'or I'll kick you in the balls.'

Whoever it was seemed to have a one-track mind. Hands gripped me by the shoulders and twisted me round several times so that I couldn't be sure which way I was facing. Then my right arm was clasped pretty firmly and he said, 'Step careful and come with me.'

'Or you'll kick me in the balls?'

'You catch on quick.'

Shuffling, I allowed myself to be led along. There was nothing else I could do. Mr X seemed a capable, single-minded individual, and if I had tried to kick out I couldn't have done much after that, with my hands tied, and blind-folded.

My first guess was that he was taking me to a car somewhere and for some obscure purpose I was being abducted. Then he guided me to the right and I recognized the distinctive smell of oil, petrol and carbon which lingers always to some degree in a well-used garage. And, as we hadn't gone more than fifty paces, it had to be mine.

Inside, he said, 'Stop! Half a pace forward.'

I did as he commanded. What the hell was he up to? A gag went round my mouth and I mmm'd protestingly.

'Shut up!' said Mr X. 'Do exactly as I say. Lift your right foot slowly.'

I lifted my right foot.

'A bit more. Now forward. Now lower it.'

My foot dropped a few inches and then rested on a firm, hard surface.

'Now lift yourself up.'

He hoisted me from behind and my shin jarred against a hard edge before my left foot joined my right. I reckoned I was standing about eighteen inches above ground. It came to me, when my knees touched some sort of frame, that I was on a chair. But even then I didn't realize until the noosed rope slipped round my neck and tightened.

My first panicky instinct was to jump back but that would have been pointless. I couldn't see, speak or move my hands. Anyway, I didn't have time for the chair was kicked from under my feet and the rope dug into my neck as my weight pulled on the noose. I was left dangling.

Fortunately the rope must have been already tight from wherever it was anchored or my neck would have probably broken, not that it made any difference.

I wasn't scared. I was petrified. I was going to die most unpleasantly. I was being garrotted.

But the instinct for survival is strong. I tensed my neck muscles as much as I could. It helped but the rope

tightened relentlessly. It hurt! God, how it hurt! I could
feel myself turning slowly like a rag doll. Inhalation was
no longer possible. I would last just as long as the oxygen
already in my lungs would let me.

My head was spinning but to the end I was keeping a
semblance of consciousness, and awareness of what was
happening, but not of time. It couldn't be long now!

Noises, funny noises! Then suddenly my hands were cut
free, the blindfold whipped off and the rope round my
arms. More noises! But my mind couldn't register any
more, and I was too far gone to lift my arms and pull on
the rope. I remember the blood pounding in my head.
Zoom! Zoom! Zoom! 'This is it!' I thought. 'This is it!'

Then strong arms grabbed my legs and lifted, my
neck was freed of the rope and I was being lowered, gasping
frantically, to the floor. There were dim shapes until
someone switched on the garage light and, as I moved to
a crouching position, I saw it was Stanford and Kendrick.

Stanford said, 'We ought to get the ambulance.'

I gulped in great lungfuls of air and, shaking my head,
I croaked, 'No. Police . . . get police!'

In five minutes I was breathing normally but I was
still shaken and my neck hurt abominably. I looked up at
the severed rope dangling from the crossbeam at the front
of my garage, but that's all there was. The ropes binding
me, the gag, they had gone. The chair lay on its side and
the loop that had been round my neck was on the floor.

I could see in their eyes that they thought I had
intended it.

'Did you see anyone?' I croaked, my voice thick and
hoarse.

They looked at me, puzzled, and shook their heads.

'We heard a bit of noise as we came up the path and
then saw you hanging there. Couldn't see it was you for
sure until we came over to you. Lucky Charlie had his
knife with him.'

Now they'd done what they could, they seemed embarrassed. I thrust my wrists at them and showed them the rope marks.

'You're thinking I tried to do myself in, aren't you? See that? See those marks? They're where somebody tied me up. He's gone and the rope's gone. Whoever it was must have heard you coming.'

They stared at me and then at each other, and I told them what had happened. I'm not sure that I fully convinced them, but we went in and I telephoned the police.

I told them I wanted Chief Superintendent Anders urgently and that he would be more annoyed than I was if they didn't get him. Events were bringing out an aggressive streak in me. After a short period of clicks, voices, clicks and voices, I was put through to a Detective-Sergeant Hudson who heard me through without interrupting. Then he said, 'Right, sir. Somebody'll be down shortly. Don't let anybody walk about outside or touch anything there.'

'They have walked about, my two friends here.'

'Well, not any more. And ask them to stay there until we arrive.' He put the phone down without waiting for further reply.

I told the others and they said they wouldn't mind staying, so we had a brandy and some coffee. Kendrick insisted on applying cold compresses to my neck because he thought it was the right thing to do, but said I was a fool not to go to hospital.

'I must say,' he said, 'after what you've been through you've recovered bloody well. I'd have been buggered.'

And I suppose it was true. Once the early paralysing nausea of shock had passed, I felt all right except for the pain in my neck. They believed me now. It must have been the way I spoke to the police.

'Who the hell would want to do that to you, John?'

I could think of only one person and I felt very sad.

The gruff voice, the crudities didn't fool me. He could do that well enough, as he could do most things. I could imagine too why he didn't want me to know who it was, even though he never expected me to be able to tell anybody.

I avoided the question. 'Thank God you arrived in time!' I said. 'But what made you come?'

Stanford cleared his throat. 'Well, after what happened and what you said in the Stag, we thought it a good idea to apologize, away from there, and to say how sorry we are about it all.'

'That's good of you.'

'We reckon we know who it was and I doubt if he'll be very welcome in future.'

'Have you asked him?'

'We're going to.'

'If he denies it, let it go. We've no proof and what's the point?'

At that moment the police came in the shape of two uniformed car patrolmen. They were in the middle of taking statements when a van arrived with plenty of equipment. Floodlights were erected all round the place and while several officers were making a search Anders drove up with two more men.

Kendrick and Stanford, who had telephoned their homes to say they would be delayed, seemed to be thoroughly enjoying it all and needed no encouragement to stay.

Immediately following Anders came another van with a dog handler and a large, formidable Alsatian dog which he held on a lead. I was standing at the door and expected Anders and his men to come inside and ply me with questions, but instead he ignored me and called out in a loud, authoritative voice, 'Everybody stay perfectly still – just where you are!'

We all froze and he then addressed me.

'Mr Bryant, I believe you said the attack first took place near your front door?'

'Yes, that's right.'

'Smethwick!' Anders called, and the dog handler came forward. The dog eyed me suspiciously. One of the officers with Anders unwrapped a polythene-covered bundle and, still holding the wrapper, let some sort of white undergarment drop on to the porch. The dog sniffed it and then ran round in circles for a short while before it appeared to pick up the scent. Then the dog, its handler and Anders went off in the direction of the garage, were lost to view for quite a while and reappeared to make a detour across the front garden to where a few cupressus bushes filled the corner. From there they went out of the front gate and down the lane to what I regard as the main road, although it isn't even classified. It was about twenty minutes before they returned. The dog jumped back into the van and Anders came up to the house.

The first thing he did was to examine my neck under the hall light.

'You've got some nasty weals there,' he said. 'You sure you're all right? Can you swallow?'

'It hurts still but I'm okay otherwise, and I've swallowed several times since.'

'No after effects – shock?'

'I think I did have, but I'm all right now.'

'You certainly had a lucky escape.'

We went into the sitting-room where I introduced him to Kendrick and Stanford. 'It seems you saved Mr Bryant from a very unpleasant end,' he said to them.

'Gives me the creeps thinking about it,' said Kendrick. 'I told him he ought to see a doctor.'

'He will do very shortly, the police surgeon.'

'Is that necessary?' I said.

'Yes, it is, for your own good and also for ours. We might need a statement from him later.' He turned to address the two uniformed officers who were standing at the back of the room. 'Where are the statements?'

'On the table, sir.'

He went over and read them, remarkably quickly, I thought.

'They'll do fine for now. We shall want more details later but you've done a good job. Now, Mr Kendrick, Mr Stanford, you haven't a car here?'

'No, we walked,' said Stanford.

'These officers will drop you home on their way to the police surgeon with Mr Bryant.'

I couldn't help admiring the definite way Anders dealt with everything.

I lingered behind after the others had got into the police car. 'Any idea who it was?' I asked him.

'Oh, yes. The same man who killed Mrs Hannaford. The dog confirmed that.'

I was intensely curious and thought I had every right to be, but he wouldn't enlarge on this statement.

Casually, perhaps too casually, I said, 'Have you seen anything of Mr Hannaford?'

He looked at me as if he were trying to see something right inside my head.

'I saw him shortly after he'd seen you,' he said, 'and the interview was very interesting. Incidentally, one of my officers will stay here with you for the night.'

My watch showed the time as five to twelve. 'Rather late for the police surgeon, isn't it?' I said.

'In our job it's never late.'

'Why do you want an officer to stay here?'

'For your protection until we've made an arrest.'

It was nearly two before we got back from the police surgeon, an abrupt, taciturn Scot who seemed more interested in making notes than in my wellbeing. He did give me some tablets in case I needed them, and told me to see my own doctor.

Smith, a solid-looking officer who had been delegated to be my bodyguard, refused the spare bed and settled in an armchair.

That night, not unnaturally, I didn't sleep much. Hannaford was on my mind all the time. My God, I thought, what happens now?

I awoke suddenly, bleary-eyed, so I must have had some sleep. It was gone nine and I went down in my dressing-gown to find that Smith, who looked a damned sight fresher than I felt, was on the phone.

'Yes, sir,' he was saying. 'Very good, sir.' He put the receiver down. 'That was Mr Anders. I can return to normal duties. They've arrested somebody.'

A sickening blanket of depression enveloped me. Almost dreading the reply, I asked, 'Who?'

'Can't say that, sir. He hasn't been charged yet but Mr Anders is satisfied that you're in no further danger.'

I got him some breakfast, and he told me about his wife and two children, when he'd joined the force and some of the things that had happened to him. He'd given up the idea of promotion as he couldn't pass the examination, but he said the CID, his section of it anyway, was a job and a half! When he mentioned Anders, I had the impression he was referring to his own personal deity. Carver, 'a tough nut' he said, could also be as soft as jelly. As he left, I realized how much I still had to learn about people, especially policemen.

I rang Hannaford's number but, as I expected, there was no answer. I rang Anders and was told he was on urgent business, so also were Carver and Hudson.

I felt restless and decided I had to do something.

I went into the studio and turned the portrait of Sally so that I could see it. Technically it was not brilliant. It was a good likeness but it lacked something. Then I looked again and the eyes began to haunt me. The half-smiling, sensual mouth seemed to want to speak. Whatever she was – good or bad – I had captured it. It was there and very disturbing. I turned it back to the wall and picked up my picture of the old mill and cottages at Copley and then, on impulse, I decided.

I had a drink and a snack in the Lion first, and when I called at the cottage with the picture under my arm, I recognized the old chap who answered the door.

'Mr Armitage?'

'Yes?' He peered at me. 'It's the artist fellow, isn't it?'

'I've brought it for you. You said you'd like to have it.'

'Yes. Yes. Come in.'

I was ushered into a cosy living-room. Light streamed from an open door on the left and from the sounds of activity there I guessed it led to the kitchen. I uncovered the painting and propped it against a wall. He nodded several times and seemed pleased.

'How much?' he asked.

'It's yours. No charge. Tell me what sort of frame you'd like and that's on me too.'

'But, young man . . .' I suppose I *was* young to him. 'Your time? This is very good of you.'

'I'm only happy that you like it.'

'Anne! Jane!' he called. 'Come and have a look at this.'

A handsome woman of about his age appeared, wiping her hands on a very clean towel. She was followed by a younger woman. I put her age at anything from thirty-five to forty-five, and it was she who took my attention. She had the most beautiful eyes I had ever seen. They had an extraordinary depth and a warmth, instantly ready, it seemed, to be compassionate. After that it was all just impressions: the regal carriage of her head, a figure the casual brown-and-green dress couldn't hide. No skin and bone here but a real woman.

'This is my wife and my daughter Jane.'

I was being thanked. Now and again I caught Jane looking at me seriously and, I thought, with interest. Yes, I said, I would be pleased to have tea with them one afternoon.

Armitage saw me to my car. 'Funny thing,' he said, 'the police came with that picture. I told them I saw you painting it and they showed me a photograph of you and I said I recognized you. Not bad for seventy-nine, eh? Was it stolen?'

'No,' I said, 'and I'm very glad it wasn't.'

I drove away and for the first time for months I experienced a feeling of tranquillity, plus a glimmer of hope for the future. The shadow of Sally's death was still there, but the sun had begun to peep round the clouds.

That evening after a rather makeshift meal I settled down with a book from the library in an endeavour to shut from my mind everything that had troubled me so much over the last few days. I wanted my brain to have a holiday. I sat in my favourite chair with a drink and began to read. It was a suspense novel by an author I'd not heard of, despite the fact that he'd apparently written about fifteen books previously, and I found it so intriguing that I couldn't put it down until I'd finished it.

It was then midnight and I went to bed. The relaxation had done me good. I slept well and felt better in the morning. The pain in my neck had decreased considerably so I cut out the idea of seeing my doctor.

I put on my dressing-gown, splashed cold water on my face as a preliminary freshener and cleaned my teeth. Then I went down, made a pot of tea and shuffled along in my slippers to get the morning paper. Beside this on the mat was a long, buff envelope. It was handwritten and addressed to me. It had been posted the previous day.

I took it, with the paper, into the sitting-room and

held it against the light. The clear, firm handwriting I knew. It was Hannaford's.

Forcing myself to keep calm, I slipped a finger along the top of the envelope. There was a long, typewritten sheet and attached to this a handwritten note:

John,

By the time you get this copy, the police will already have had the original. I shan't see you again.

Good luck, and thank you for being such a good friend.

Tom

I sank into a chair and read the copy, which was a professionally-worded statement. The date, time and his address were given in the top right-hand corner. Then:

My name is Thomas Charles Hannaford, and I make this statement of my own free will while of sound mind, without duress or encouragement, in order to clear my friend, John Bryant, of any implication in the death of Clarence Cunningham.

I met Cunningham about fifteen years ago when I was on holiday in France. At first I liked him and we formed a business partnership. Later I broke this off as I detected an unscrupulous and mean streak in him.

About five years ago I learned that he had gone into the property market and that he was 'legally' swindling gullible persons, especially in the purchase of Spanish properties. I made it my business to find out more about his activities. Not surprisingly, I found that he had invested a large portion of his fraudulent profits in diamonds which he always carried on his person. From my previous association with him I had a good idea where this would be.

I decided to deprive him of most of the diamonds, keep some of these for myself and recompense anonymously those of his victims I could trace.

About eighteen months ago I formed a firm friendship with Mr John Bryant, and I rented a furnished property at Marchester in his name but without his knowing it. Forging his signature, I wrote to Cunningham, telling him I was interested in his proposition of investments in Spain. By this means I lured him to Marchester and, with the help of an accomplice, whom I shall not name, I satisfied him that 'Mr Bryant' would be willing to part with a hundred pounds as part payment of the deal. My accomplice, posing as Mr Bryant, came to an arrangement with him and gave him a cheque. I had acquired Mr Bryant's chequebook without his knowledge and had returned it with one cheque missing. I had to have a bona fide chequebook holder, as the cheque had to be cancelled later.

As expected, Cunningham was delighted with the outcome of his visit and my accomplice gave him a drink as he was about to depart. I knew he would ask for gin and tonic, and this he did. The drink was laced with a slow-acting drug and as I had let down the tyre of his car while he was inside, he was delayed long enough for the drink to take effect. While he was unconscious I found, as expected, the diamonds on his person and I replaced half of them with good paste samples. The ambulance was then sent for and he was taken to hospital. My accomplice, after cancelling the cheque by telephone, drove his car and I drove Cunningham's car to the hospital. My action over the cheque explains why Mr Bryant has expressed ignorance of it.

I did not expect Cunningham to trade in the diamonds for some time, but unfortunately he attempted to do so. His suspicions were aroused and this led him to trace the real Mr John Bryant, who knew nothing about it at all.

On the 10th August I called at Mr Bryant's house and immediately noticed that his garage doors were open and the garage empty. I remembered then that he'd said he might be going to Copley to paint the old mill there. But outside his house was a car which I recognized as Cunningham's. The fact that Mr Bryant's car was missing and Cunningham's car was there made me suspicious, so I went quietly round to the back of the house. It was then I found that a pane of glass in the back door was broken and the door unlocked. I went inside. I heard someone moving about in the sitting-room. It was Cunningham.

The conversation between us isn't important. He became aggressive and I struck him, causing him to fall across the fireplace. By sheer chance his head with his full weight behind it must have landed on a fire-iron. Anyway it didn't take me long to establish that he was dead.

I dragged him to the rug, which was stupid of me because blood seeped on to it. After some thought I decided what to do. Whatever happened, I didn't want to involve Mr Bryant. I got a canvas sheet from my car, wrapped Cunningham's body in it and put it in the boot of his car and locked it. Then I washed the rug and the fire-iron, and drove Cunningham's car to Whittingham Gorge where I parked it in the woods. I practically ran to Selford where I got a bus back to Fellingbridge and walked to Mr Bryant's place. He still hadn't returned home.

I drove my own car to my shop, told my manager, Mr Chapman, that I had to go to London and suggested he close early as there was very little business that day. Then I drove to the Gorge, put Cunningham's body in the driving seat of his car, which was difficult as he was now rather stiff, and staged the accident. I spent the night in London. I didn't expect anybody to find the car until the following day at the earliest when the time of death would be more difficult to establish.

This is a true statement. Mr Bryant knows nothing of this, but I feel that now the police have proved that Cunningham was killed in his house he will, without this confession, always be under suspicion.

If you look to the left near the road in a direct line to where the car with Cunningham's body was found, you will see buried under leaves the canvas sheet in which I wrapped the body. I hope this will prove that this statement is true.

Thomas Hannaford

It was now clear to me at last why Hannaford had faked the break-in, why he had impressed on me the urgency of keeping up a pretence of ignorance come what may, why I'd had to discover the break when I got home, why I'd had to go to a place like Copley and work on an identifiable landscape.

He had planned cleverly against the possibility of the police ever connecting me and my cottage with Cunningham and the house at Marchester. Someone could have seen Cunningham's car near or at the cottage or Cunningham could have asked about me. For my protection he had tried to back events both ways.

However, this may have been before he had discovered about Sally and me. I had never established exactly when she was supposed to have disappeared. I visualized a stormy meeting between them, and if he lost his temper – slow to anger people are always worse when that happens – he could have killed her. He was unusually powerful. And then when he had called, dejected and apologetic, to tell me that she was missing, that he knew all about our relationship and didn't blame me, that could have been a set-up, a piece of good acting in preparation for pinning her death on me.

But why had he now changed his mind? The only thing I could think of was that he had learned that his attempt to fake my suicide – the last act of a conscience-stricken person – had failed and this, together with his imminent arrest, had made him think again.

At that moment I had an impulse to drive to the Armitages' cottage. I don't know why. With hindsight, I suppose subconsciously I felt that I would find emotional sanctuary there. But I didn't go. I didn't know what to do so I did nothing.

I washed, shaved and dressed, and then just sat around or walked about the garden.

What surprised me was that there was nothing about the previous night's episode in the newspaper. I should have thought this would have brought the reporters running. Later I was to discover that Kendrick and Stanford had been told to say nothing about it to anybody.

I don't know what I should have done eventually that day if Anders hadn't rung. It was about two o'clock.

'How d'you feel?' he asked. 'Have you seen your doctor?'

'No. I don't think it's necessary and I've already seen yours.'

'It's rather important that *you* see *me* as soon as possible. I'd appreciate it if you could come straight away. Hope you don't mind?'

'I don't mind,' I said. 'I'm past minding anything.'

Anders had a very nice office, with a large, flat-topped oak desk instead of one of those modern tin things. I sat in a comfortable armchair facing him.

'I'm hoping you may be able to help us,' he said. 'We

are trying to find Mr Hannaford. It seems that he has made it his business to disappear.'

This completely threw me. 'But I thought . . .'

'What did you think?'

'I thought you had arrested him.'

'What for?'

'For killing his wife and attacking me. Isn't that why you withdrew your officer from guarding me?'

'We've arrested a man for murdering Mrs Hannaford and for attacking you, but it wasn't Mr Hannaford.'

'But . . . but who . . .?'

'A man will be charged shortly after you leave here. His name is Clive Chapman. He managed Mr Hannaford's antique business.'

I was astounded and said so.

'I must admit,' said Anders, 'that he was the last person we suspected until Mr Hannaford came to see me. But this is away from the point at the moment. Have you any idea at all where we might find Mr Hannaford?'

'If he's not at home or at his shop, I haven't the faintest,' I said, which of course was perfectly true.

He went 'Hmm!' and then, with an air which suggested we both enjoyed a confidence, he said, 'About this confession of his . . .'

It was a clever move and I must have given myself away because I couldn't have looked sufficiently surprised. All I said was 'Confession?' and stuttered slightly.

He gazed at me as if he knew I was deceiving him but understood. After a pause he said, 'He didn't tell you then what he was going to do, or let you know afterwards?'

'I don't know what you're talking about,' I said, in control once more. 'What has he confessed to?'

'I received a statement from him this morning. He says that he was responsible for Cunningham's death and faking the accident. It was quite detailed and conclusive and it exonerates you completely.'

'Can I see it – the statement?'

He slid open a drawer and passed the original to me.

'No reason why you shouldn't,' he said.

I read it carefully as if I had never seen it before, conscious that he was watching me all the time. Then I gave it back to him.

'That is amazing. Did you find the canvas sheet?'

'Yes, more or less where he said it would be. I find a lot of things about this "amazing", Mr Bryant, including Mr Hannaford himself. An extraordinary man. I must say I liked him.'

'Liked?' I said. 'D'you mean you think he's dead?'

'No. But I doubt whether he'll appear again if we don't find him. He would have to answer charges and, if I'm not mistaken, a few pertinent questions about some other matters.'

Here he tried to stare me down again and I thought it expedient to change the subject.

'You say he came to see you and it was after that you suspected Chapman?'

'I didn't suspect him very strongly even then, but he did. Apparently you told Mr Hannaford about the phone call we'd had concerning your affair with Mrs Hannaford and that you had been to Copley. He said that *he'd* told Chapman you had gone there and he placed a lot of significance on this, although I can't see why. Anybody could have seen you there or Chapman could have mentioned it to someone. Can you throw any light on it?'

If Chapman had been the only person he'd told, that made just the three of us who knew, apart from the unlikely event of anybody else sufficiently interested finding out by sheer chance. But I couldn't understand why Chapman had murdered Sally or had made the phone call.

I shook my head and said nothing.

'I told him we wanted a little more than that,' continued Anders, 'and reluctantly he volunteered the information that Chapman had been having an affair with his wife for some time.'

I suddenly felt unclean.

'Him too!' I said.

'That's what Mr Hannaford alleged. He wouldn't say any more except that if we didn't do something about it he would take the law into his own hands. I told him that of course we would follow any new lead, and this we did.

'I went to the shop in the afternoon and, although I didn't get very far with Chapman, I sensed something wrong. For one thing he denied having an affair with Mrs Hannaford and I had a strong feeling he was lying. As a result of this, we re-introduced house-to-house enquiries near the Hannafords' house and found someone we had missed previously. He had seen a car in the runway and it roughly fitted the description of Chapman's car.'

He had been stuffing tobacco into the bowl of his pipe as he was talking, and he put a flame from his lighter to it and puffed. I was too sick inside to do or say anything, and he must have noticed this for he said, 'D'you feel all right?'

'No. I can't say that I do but go on, please.'

'We went to his house in the evening several times, but he wasn't at home. I left two officers to keep watch there. Then the message came through about the attack on you and I gave instructions for forced entry and for suitable scent articles to be removed. The rest you know. When Chapman returned home two of my men were waiting for him.

'He has admitted everything, including the fact that Mrs Hannaford told him that she had transferred her affections to you and had taunted him about you. He knew Mr Hannaford was in London that night so he called on her. They had an argument and it ended in a hysterical outburst from her, during which he lost his head and strangled her. Knowing you had been to Copley, he dumped her there to throw suspicion on you and later telephoned us to make sure we knew you'd gone there. When you were released, he realized that his plan had misfired, so he attempted to stage what would appear to be your suicide as a proof of your guilt.'

Anders glanced at his watch. 'Is there anything you would like to tell me now?'

'Nothing. I just feel bloody awful about it all.'

'I liked Mr Hannaford. He seemed highly intelligent and of strong character. Why would such a man allow his wife to have one affair with an employee and another with a friend and do nothing about it? It doesn't make sense.'

'It doesn't make sense to me either.'

'I have learned never to be surprised at anything, but I like to tie up the ends when I can. I suppose you wouldn't like to clear up another query for me?'

'If I can.'

'The cheque that is missing, the letter from the bank and the reply in your name with your signature, do you still maintain you knew nothing about them?'

'I do.'

He didn't believe me, of course, and as I was about to leave he said, 'I wonder, Mr Bryant, who Mr Hannaford's accomplice was!'

CHAPTER XI

I stood outside the police headquarters hearing and yet not hearing the urban sounds around me. It was as if I were on a different plane from the people who passed by and from the swishing tyres and droning of motor traffic on the road ahead.

This had been the last scene of the last act and any moment the curtain would come down. But the principal actors would not appear to take their bow.

Perhaps I had missed a point somewhere along the way, for the ending hadn't been quite clear to me. There were too many unanswered questions, but I wasn't yet in the frame of mind to grapple with them. My car, standing where I had left it, provided the only touch of reality and I suddenly felt a genuine affection for it.

Away from the town I began to think again without it hurting, but I didn't go straight home. I parked near the river and walked along the towpath.

Hannaford had told Chapman I was going to Copley. Why? The answer came suddenly, a common sense one. He would have brought it up casually, hoping that it would partly corroborate and help to strengthen my alibi if one were ever needed. At the same time no doubt he had mentioned that he would be staying in London for the night. Then when he'd heard about the phone call to the police he had realized that Chapman was the only one apart from ourselves who knew. Maybe other things had come back to him for, according to Anders, he had been quite sure of Chapman's guilt.

The big mystery was Hannaford himself. As Anders had said, knowing what his wife was up to, why hadn't he done something about it? And why had infidelity been such a casual thing where she was concerned? Her death had shaken him so he must have felt deeply about her.

As for me, I should never be quite the same again, which perhaps wasn't a bad thing. With sadness I remembered the note he had sent me with the copy of his statement. '. . . *I shan't see you again. Good luck, and thank you for being such a good friend.*'

'*I shan't see you again!*' It had a hollow ring to it. One line from a French poem came aptly to my mind. '*Partir c'est mourir un peu.*' To part is to die a little!

That was how I felt about Hannaford.

I sat on the bank and watched the smooth-running stream and listened to its soft tinkling murmur. As I had done many times before, I noticed its changing shades of colour, the occasional plops and ripples as perhaps a fish or some water insect disturbed the surface. I was more conscious than ever of the delicate fresh fragrance of the grasses and reeds. It had always been a tranquil, soothing place but for me never so much as now.

I lit my pipe and smoked it through before I went back to my car and drove home.

I can never accept the so-called metaphysical. However strange it may seem, there is in my opinion a scientific explanation. Such things as extra-sensory perception, telepathy, premonitions which come true – and of course those which don't – all have a rational explanation which will sooner or later be discovered by somebody. Man has always been too ready to attribute supernatural causes to phenomena he can't understand.

Having said this, I will admit that as soon as I had shut the front door behind me I experienced a weird, prickling sensation I had never known before. Everything was dead quiet and there was, I felt sure, somebody else in the cottage. Then, as if guided there, I went straight to my studio and turned the portrait of Sally so that it faced me.

I stood without moving, the silence pressing on me from all sides. Everything else round me faded. The lips I had painted, and which had once before seemed on the point of speaking, now spoke. They didn't move but the message came across. The eyes expressed the thoughts behind them. The face and body, which before had held so powerful an attraction for me, filled me with revulsion.

Now I knew! I knew it all!

'I hate my husband,' she was saying. 'I hate him but I love him. He is mine. No one else shall claim his affections, especially other men. I will destroy them and him if necessary. I know that sometimes I am mad, but it's the way I was born. I know too that he only tolerates me now. But he still loves me. Whatever I do, he'll never leave me because that's the way *he* is.'

The eyes seemed to change slightly, revealing the derangement and the obsession in the brain no human hand could have painted unaided.

I shivered and shouted, 'Witch! Witch!' Then in almost feverish haste I grabbed the portrait and ran to the incinerator at the end of the garden. There I watched it burn and stayed until it was a heap of ashes.

I breathed deeply as I walked slowly back to the house. I opened all the windows and doors. I didn't go near the drinks cabinet. Instead I put on a record and sat and listened to a Mozart piano concerto.

When it was finished, I felt that the house was free of her and that I was my own man again.

I felt too that I knew Hannaford better than I had ever done. He lived mainly by his own laws which were black and white, with not much grey in between. For normal human failings he made allowances, yet he abhorred hypocrisy. When he thought it appropriate he could, under the cover of a practical, carefree approach, be extremely compassionate. He had loved his wife to the end, even when he must have known that her pathological and possessive self-love had disturbed the balance of her mind.

The details of their relationship, how and when it had all gone wrong, I would probably never know, but I was in no doubt that it was his compassion that had kept them together.

I suppose neither of them had behaved normally – if there is such a thing as normality. And who was I to criticize? I had come out of it badly. I was indeed ashamed.

The only excuse I could allow myself was perhaps that I too, if not temporarily insane, had come under an irresistible power beyond my understanding. I would never again feel sure what a human being might or might not do in given circumstances.

I saw Anders only once again, a few days later when we went over possible charges against Chapman for attempted murder. At my insistence it was agreed not to press them unless he changed his plea concerning Sally.

After that the police didn't bother me any more. I half expected to be called for the inquest on Cunningham but I wasn't. I read about it in the newspapers and my name was mentioned in rather sensational accounts in two of them. The rug and fire-iron were produced and Hannaford's written confession. I'd already told the police I didn't want the rug and fire-iron back and that they could stick them in their museum or do what they liked with them.

Unfortunately that wasn't quite the end of the affair, because reporters kept coming round, photographing the place and asking questions. But by now I had acquired a harder crust and I refused to comment.

I went away for a month, wandering through France and Italy, at the end of which time it had all quietened down. There was still Chapman's trial to come but apart from being the unwitting cause of his jealousy I wasn't involved.

On the second day back I remembered old Armitage saying I'd be welcome for afternoon tea, so I telephoned first and drove over.

That was eighteen months ago and a great deal has happened since then. Chapman got life and, although the intimacies between Sally and myself were not spelled out in detail, I came in for some unwelcome publicity again.

This worried me no end because I thought it might affect my friendship with the Armitages which had blossomed considerably. But I had already told them some of the story and they were more concerned for me than anything.

Jane and I were married six months ago. Unlike my previous experiences which had exploded into immediate intensity, the relationship between us developed gradually. She, I discovered, had been unhappily married several years previously and, although she refrained from condemning her former husband outright, I read between the lines and placed him as a suave, foot-loose scoundrel. However, just as divorce proceedings were pending, he had the decency to get himself killed in a fracas abroad.

This rather explained to me her equally cautious approach, but as we saw more and more of each other I detected an affinity between us. Little by little the barriers were dismantled until one day I felt compelled to tell her everything. And knowing that I was taking a risk in doing so, I left out nothing.

For several fateful moments she was silent. Then tenderly she took my face between her hands and kissed me. We clung together and, when we drew away and I saw the tears on her cheeks, I knew they were tears of happiness.

If I am sure of anything, it is that this time I've made no mistake. I remember Hannaford saying that really deep platonic affection can transcend sexual desire. In our case I think we have both. Ironically, if it hadn't been for Hannaford and all that happened to me because of him, I should never have met her.

I often think of Hannaford and wonder what he's doing and where he is. To date the police haven't found him and I doubt if they ever will.

Jane has just come in from the village. She kisses me on

the cheek and ruffles my hair, and then drops a letter on to the table.

'That was on the door mat,' she says.

The postmark is practically indecipherable but there is an Italian stamp. My name and address are typewritten.

Opening it, I take out a colour photograph, and there is Hannaford in swimming trunks, bronzed, athletic, looking perhaps a little older but still with that kindly, whimsical smile. In the background there is nothing to identify the location and I'm damned sure he is nowhere near Italy now.

There is also a handwritten note:

Congratulations, John, on your marriage. The best of luck. You really deserve it.

You'll be pleased to know the Steer brought a good price, half of which I sent on to the old lady's sister. I wonder what our doctor got for yours?

Distance can't sever real friendships. They stay in the heart for ever. Thank you for yours.

Tom

I can feel a deep rush of emotion spreading over me. I am trying to fight it. But why should I?

Jane has come back into the room and I pass the note and photograph to her. She has finished the note now. 'He must be a most unusual man,' she says.

I take her hand for comfort. 'He is! He is!'